An Old Man's Diary

The Italian Problem in European Diplomacy 1847–49
Germany's First Bid for Colonies, 1884–85
The Course of German History
The Habsburg Monarchy, 1809–1918
From Napoleon to Stalin
Rumours of War
The Struggle for Mastery in Europe 1848–1918
(The Oxford History of Modern Europe)
Bismarck: The Man and the Statesman
Englishmen and Others
The Troublemakers
The Origins of the Second World War
The First World War
Politics in Wartime
English History, 1914–1945
(The Oxford History of England)
From Sarajevo to Potsdam
Europe: Grandeur and Decline
(Penguin: Selected Essays)
War by Time-Table
Beaverbrook
The Second World War
Essays in English History
The Last of Old Europe
The War Lords
The Russian War, 1941–1945
How Wars Begin
Revolutions and Revolutionaries
Politicians, Socialism and Historians
A Personal History

Edited by A. J. P. Taylor

Lloyd George, A Diary by Frances Stevenson
Off the Record by W. P. Crozier
My Darling Pussy, the Letters of
Lloyd George and Frances Stevenson

A. J. P. TAYLOR

An Old Man's Diary

HAMISH HAMILTON

LONDON

First published in Great Britain 1984
by Hamish Hamilton Ltd
Garden House, 57–59 Long Acre, London WC2E 9JZ

British Library Cataloguing in Publication Data

Taylor, A. J. P.
    An old man's diary—
    1. Taylor, A. J. P.   2. Historians – Great
    Britain – Correspondence, reminiscence, etc.
    I. Title
    907'.2024   D15.T/
    ISBN 0-241-11247-8

Typeset by Rowland Phototypesetting Ltd
Bury St Edmunds, Suffolk
Printed in Great Britain by
St Edmundsbury Press, Bury St Edmunds, Suffolk

Contents

Foreword

The contents of this book do not really make up a Diary in the conventional sense. In my youth I kept a genuine diary for some ten years. Then I decided that keeping it was occupying too much of my time. Also too many people knew of its existence. So I ceased to write any more and destroyed all of it to my subsequent regret. Many years later, in November 1980, Anthony Howard invited me to write the Langham Diary occasionally for *The Listener* and a year or so later Karl Miller induced me to move over to *The London Review of Books* where I still am. My writings are passing comments on events and on my own life, not a systematic diary. I regret only one entry. That was my first reaction to the Argentine invasion of the Falklands which I condemned with a patriotic fervour worthy of Mrs Thatcher or Michael Foot. By the next occasion I wrote on this topic I condemned the war as firmly as Dr Johnson had condemned a similar war some two hundred years before.

As a bonus I have added the Romanes Lecture for 1981 (academic year) which I gave at the Sheldonian Theatre, Oxford, in March 1982. The Romanes Lecture is the most prestigious lecture in the gift of Oxford University and I am deeply grateful to my old friend and colleague Geoffrey Warnock for presenting it to me. The Romanes Lecture has proved my last lecture and is I think my best.

I thank the editors of *The Listener* and *The London Review of Books* for publishing the instalments of my Diary. I also thank *The London Review of Books* for publishing my Romanes Lecture from a tape. It was of course given without either notes or a script.

I

Langham Diary, *The Listener*

1

On Monday I rounded off my autumnal forays of lecturing by a visit to the Birmingham branch of the Historical Association. Such visits are the only occasions when I lecture purely for pleasure, or maybe with a touch of missionary zeal to keep up interest in history for its own sake. If this interest were not maintained, who would read my books, let alone buy them?

My visits have another practical use; they give me a cast-iron excuse for refusing invitations from anyone else. Dining clubs, worthy causes, university Unions, college history societies all receive a printed card of regret, somewhat hypocritical, together with a scrawled addition, 'branches of the Historical Association only'. On reflection I think my refusals fully justified. I am not a public entertainer, though some try to cast me for that role. University students should receive adequate instruction from their professors without my assistance. As to the worthy causes, from the anti-fluoride society to CND, I doubt whether they benefit from meetings where the converted address the converted with passionate rhetoric. In any case, I have had enough of trying to save the world from destruction. Let the gallant champions of democracy and communism and whatever else is around blow themselves and everyone else sky-high if that is what they feel like. I had rather stick to branches of the Historical Association.

*

Now happily back in my retirement in North London, I contemplate gloomily what I am to say about the various products of the BBC. There is a prior problem – what are the current products? I am what might be called a devoted non-viewer and non-listener – except for music, I have the correct devices for viewing television and listening to radio. But I rarely turn them on. Indeed, I am not

3

sure I can turn on the television. These devices are my equivalent of the monarch – Roman emperor or Prussian king – who kept a mistress for ostentation, not for use. I resisted colour television for years and have now succumbed. Deeply do I repent this. The so-called controls are baffling, at least uncontrollable by me. On the rare occasions when the device works, the colours shown are hideous beyond description. All the human faces are bright red – the men's, I assume, from alcoholism, the women's, I hope, from shame at taking part in such an exhibition.

As to the radio, which is also my gramophone, it demands two loudspeakers, which dominate the room. To appreciate them, it seems, I have to sit equidistant between them, which makes it impossible for anyone else to use the room, or at any rate to listen. I am told that the reproduction is now indistinguishable from the real thing, which is nonsense. All reproduction is mechanical, accustoming you to the work performed, but with no aesthetic merit. The best reproduction I ever heard came from a gramophone with an enormous papier mâché horn which I possessed in the Thirties. It transcended all stereos and was worth the trouble of changing the record every four and a half minutes, to say nothing of clipping the thorn needle with special scissors.

*

To write so slightingly of these radiophonic miracles is, I suppose, to bite the hand that feeds me – or has fed me so lavishly in the past. Just on 40 years ago (March or April 1941, I think) I gave my first radio talk. Slightly over 30 years ago (August 1950) I first appeared in that now-legendary television programme, *In the News*, along with Michael Foot and others. Now these ghosts rise up to haunt me. Last week I had to get up early in order to join Michael and Malcolm Muggeridge on a radio programme called *Start the Week*. With both, my friendship goes back into the mists of antiquity. I had read that both had achieved positions of great public importance – Malcolm as a spiritual leader, Michael as a statesman of the first rank. Maybe, I thought, they will not recognise me; certainly they will have forgotten the gay hours we passed together. Not at all. They were both unchanged in spirit, and even in looks, at any rate to my bedazzled eyes. I hope they thought the same of me. I noticed that they had both retained at its ripest the radio technique which is known, in the parlance of the trade, as 'hogging the mike'. I spent most of my time silent, in a state of bemused admiration. At least, that is how it seemed to me. A highly qualified listener – my wife, of course – told me I had said quite a lot and that what I said was much more cogent than the passionate oratory of the other contenders. No wonder I like to spend so much of my days at home.

*

Television is a different matter. I make an exception of keeping the television set switched off and always watch my own appearances if the knobs allow me to. I invented the art of unscripted television lectures as long ago as 1957. I was told then that it would not work and have often been told it since. But so far it seems to have worked all right, despite occasional bans, political or technical. It is fascinating to watch a television personality of one's own name. I have nothing in common with the screen figure whom I think of vaguely as Him. He has mannerisms which had never occurred to me. He says things that astonish me – sometimes penetrating remarks that I should never have hit on, sometimes rash generalisations that seem to me a trifle unscholarly – but he always seems to pull through somehow. Occasionally I think of something he ought to say and is going to miss. Just when I have despaired of Him, he says it after all. I rather like Him, though I am glad I am not Him or anything like it in real life.

The other thing I like when I am lecturing is the camera. I treat it as a living person and talk to it as I would to a friend sitting in my room – a bit more formally, of course, but with a recognition that it is as much alive as I am. I try to follow the rule given to me by my tutor, G. N. Clark, years ago: 'Say simple things to simple men.' That is easy, because I am simple myself. If I have another guiding principle as an historian, it is 'The Emperor has no clothes'. Critics complain that I am a debunking historian. I prefer to think that I am a realist, except in the way I envy Him, my television double.

*

And now, having written unflatteringly of those scientific marvels radio and television, I sing the praise of an older technical triumph, now 150 years old, the railways. While road traffic gets worse,

5

railways get better. They are faster, they are cleaner, they are more agreeable. The sensation of effortless speed, passing through a countryside that appears mostly unspoilt, is magical. The historic stations, when preserved, are still glamorous, with a special word of praise for that masterpiece of Gilbert Scott's, St Pancras. The story that it was first prepared as a design for the Foreign Office is apparently a legend, and a good thing too – the Foreign Office did not deserve it. The new Euston is lamentable, and very inconvenient into the bargain. When I said that the stones in the great monument, the Gateway to the North, had been dispersed, I was told that it was built of brick. I had grave qualms of conscience, only to learn that I had been right after all. This often happens with me.

2

The new session of Parliament is now in full swing or, alternatively, total stagnation. Choose whichever phrase you like; they mean much the same thing. The explanation of this strange condition has only just occurred to me. No one has the slightest idea what to do and no one knows what he is doing. The politicians use phrases that mean nothing even to themselves. Economists propound rival remedies which, added together, all come to the same answer: zero. The Red Queen at least managed to remain in the same place by running very fast. Our mentors and guides have us slithering steadily backwards the harder they make us run. We are assured that inflation will come down a little. No one suggests that it should be halted altogether. Yet inflation was until recently the most pressing social evil. Now unemployment has taken its place and all we are promised in the most cheerful tones is that it will soon be much greater – 'up and up and on and on and on', as Ramsay MacDonald said, with equal fatuity, on a similar occasion. We are heading for a society where everyone will be out of work except for Ministers and MPs and where no one will be able to buy anything because the prices will be too high. I am simple-minded enough to dream that there must be a remedy somewhere. After all, the Roman emperors at Constantinople held the purchasing power of the gold byzant stable for 800 years. Then the Crusaders wrecked that great enterprise. They stole the four horses of St Mark's; they did not discover the secret of the byzant. Nor will our rulers or their opponents.

*

There is another activity of our rulers which, in its bare-faced effrontery, I almost admire. This is shown in their latest precautions against a nuclear war. Until recently they claimed to have a 'second strike' strategy, a power of retaliation or, as it was optimistically called, deterrence. Now they, like others, are embarked on the 'first-strike' strategy, an attack so hard and so great that there can be no response. Our rulers bravely face the consequences. They assure us that a nuclear war by this country will preserve 15 million survivors. So 40 million will have been killed. It seems incredible that any sane leader can even contemplate such a figure, but so it is. I am interested in the survivors. How will they be chosen? Will it be purely by chance or will there be some design? Apparently it will be the latter. Nuclear-proof residences are being provided underground for the chosen few. And, of course, those who do the choosing have naturally chosen themselves. There will be the Royal Family; the Prime Minister and her colleagues; and the defence chiefs, particularly those concerned with nuclear weapons. What an extraordinary coincidence. The very people who have led us to the slaughterhouse are to be preserved in the hope of repeating their achievement. I had understood that the captain was always the last to leave his sinking ship, if indeed he did not go down with it. This example does not inspire the present dictators of our policy. No nonsense about 'women and children first' for them. However, I don't worry. The fate of those who survive a nuclear war is likely to be much more unpleasant than the fate of the 40 million who are killed by it.

*

I have long suspected that most people cannot read. Recently I have modified my view. Now I think that many people, when asked or instructed to do one thing, automatically do the opposite. Take, for instance, the notices displayed in the passages of London's Underground: KEEP TO THE LEFT. Everyone, without exception, keeps to the right in every passage. Such uniformity can only be an organised display of high-minded anarchism. So I keep right also. The notices on the top deck of London buses provide an equally interesting example. They read: SMOKERS ARE ASKED TO OCCUPY REAR SEATS. That would seem to be a fair compromise between the needs of smokers and of non-smokers, rather too generous to the smokers, I should say. What happens? Those who intend to smoke direct their steps to the front seats, preferably those right at the front. The offenders are mainly women, ranging from schoolgirls

8

to those of a respectable middle age. Does this show that women are more anarchic than men? Another curious feature is that most women, having lit a cigarette and taken one puff, then hold the cigarette between finger and thumb until it has smouldered away. If they draw on it at all, this is followed by a puff of smoke directed at the notice facing them. Most dramatic of all is the notice on every cigarette packet as a warning from the government: CIGARETTES CAN SERIOUSLY DAMAGE YOUR HEALTH. I suspect that this is the most effective advertising slogan ever invented.

*

Thirty years ago I spent many happy days at the Public Record Office in Chancery Lane. The procedure was delightfully un-changed from the 19th century. You filled up a large form with the significant number, handed it in and then waited half an hour or so until the volume was delivered to you by a uniformed attendant. As you were allowed only three volumes of documents at a time there were many happy intervals when you could read the news-papers or survey the more attractive women researchers. Now all is changed: the modern documents have been removed to Kew and computerised. When I tried to obtain a document I was offered for some reason a bleeper. This alarmed me so much that I fled from Kew and abandoned research for ever. I was consoled that the mediaeval documents had remained at Chancery Lane and were delivered with the old formalities. Now I learn that even the researchers into mediaeval history will have to travel to Kew. What will happen to the real Record Office in Chancery Lane? I hope it will be preserved unchanged with its long, reverberating corridors and its director's room almost as large as that allotted to re-searchers. The Fetter Lane front, rarely seen, is a late masterpiece by Sir James Pennethorne; the Chancery Lane extension by Sir John Taylor some 40 years later. May both wings long survive.

*

Reviewers sometimes recall Macaulay when reviewing some book or other of mine. Embarrassed by the comparison, I have begun to read Macaulay's *History of England* and am as bewitched as I was when I first read it some 55 years ago. I had expected the style to be rather old-fashioned, almost Gibbonian. Not at all. There are

9

more single-verb sentences one after another than I should ever dare to attempt. Macaulay invented the Bren-gun-style long before I did and used it far more ruthlessly. Another thing I had forgotten were the allusions to contemporary events which I should not venture on: wise words on Catholic Emancipation, a penetrating analysis of the Irish question and a correct demonstration that Torbay was a pleasanter place in the 19th century than it had been when William the Deliverer landed there. The essays are a different matter: mostly reviews hastily written and over-emphatic, as I dare say mine are. I do not say Macaulay was the greatest of historians, only that he was a very great one.

3

To number a distinguished public figure among one's personal friends has its embarrassments. I have known Michael Foot almost as long as I can remember. We marched and orated together in the old days of CND. In the Fifties we sat side by side in many television debates with Michael exclaiming 'Stabbed in the back again' when I deviated from the Labour Party line. I never expected to give evidence on his behalf as though he were an aspiring academic hoping to become a professor. But now radio and television producers, journalists and political pundits, to say nothing of foreign observers, all ask me: 'Will Foot make a good leader of the Labour Party?' I am tempted to reply, 'How on earth should I know? I am not in the political trade.' I am delighted at an old friend's success. As a humble member of the Labour Party since 1921 I think he is more likely than anyone else to hold the party together. Many people regard Michael as simply a great agitator. There is much more to him. Beneath his polemical exterior he is a first-rate executive. He was a successful editor of the *Evening Standard* at its best. He kept *Tribune* going through many crises. Above all, he believes in the finest principles of the Labour Party. It is often thought that the Labour leader must be a moderate. Not at all. George Lansbury was a great leader of the party in the dark years between 1931 and 1935. Clem Attlee, despite his seeming moderation, once said to me, 'I hate the Tories.' So does Michael. I have every confidence in his leadership, though no doubt a time will come when I shall disagree with him. Then Michael will say once more, 'Stabbed in the back again.'

*

The year 1980 is drawing to its close. I must polish up my list of possible lectures for 1981. I like anniversaries – centenaries or

11

shorter ten-year periods. 1880 provided a whole run of lectures in itself. Before that were the Bulgarian Horrors (1876) and the Congress of Berlin (1878). But 1881 looks pretty barren. Gladstone's second Irish Land Bill won't do, though the death of Disraeli, Earl of Beaconsfield, might provide an occasional topic. The Bradlaugh case was running hard throughout the early 1880s, but with nothing sensational in 1881. I can think of nothing for 1781 or for 1681 either. Trying shorter periods, there is of course 1931, but the doings of Ramsay MacDonald and others in that year will be overdone without any assistance from me. But what about cheating and falling back on 75 years? That gives 1906, a wonderful year. The Liberals won their finest victory. Lloyd George and Churchill both took their first steps to greatness. I was born in 1906 and so was the Historical Association. I can lecture without shame about my own career and my modest contributions to the art of history. Meanwhile, the Historical Association is preparing celebrations on a grand scale. Leading historians are to be drawn in to lecture at every great city in the country and in small towns also. In November, I shall lecture at a culminating meeting in the Museum of London, my topic, I think, the year 1906 itself. The political themes are easy but there is much else. What important books were published in 1906? What inventions were made, a subject I am weak on? I must go cap in hand for suggestions.

*

The mention of my birth in 1906 reminds me that I have not all that much time left. What have I left undone that I can do in my remaining years? It is too late to start on any mountain area I don't know. I had better just stick to the Lake District and renew acquaintance with the less formidable fells. But there must surely be new sights to see. One ambition is still alive for me: I really must go to Autun. I once spent a night there, but as it was the night of 2 September 1939 I did not see much. It would be a great misfortune to miss the first signed sculptures in mediaeval Europe. I am in process of fulfilling a long-cherished wish by hearing all the Beethoven Quartets in the series that the Amadeus Quartet have just begun at the Queen Elizabeth Hall, an experience that in itself makes life worth living. *The Blue Angel* at the National Film Theatre – certainly not, once is quite enough. But I can take as

12

many W. C. Fields films as there are on offer. What novels should I read again? *David Copperfield* and *The Mayor of Casterbridge* of course. Scott? I think *Old Mortality*, though not all Scott lovers rate it as highly as I do. I should like to reread *The Diary of a Nobody*, but I have mislaid my copy. Probably some member of my family has made off with it. And I should like to write a book on the Cold War, but that is a subject that has caused me too much trouble already. I might write my autobiography. At present I can think of no more than the title: *An Uninteresting Story*. I expect I shall have enough to do without bothering about that.

*

There is one little puzzle in contemporary life that I am unable to solve: why are addresses so much longer than they used to be? I don't mean public speeches. I never read them. No, I mean what I write on an envelope. It used to be easy: name of recipient; number of house and road; name of place. Now you usually begin with some department and follow that with the institution concerned. Most departments and indeed many individuals live in a house, to be followed with a street and a number. Then come name of place, county and at the end a jumble of figures and capital letters. What is it all for? When I set up in a new house some three years ago I asked at the local post office for my postal code and duly used it conscientiously. Then another government department told me I had been using the wrong code. Yet my letters had all been reaching me more or less punctually and they reached me no more punctually when I switched over to the right code. Perhaps it is wrong too. My mind is stuffed with numbers – postal code, National Health number, National Insurance number (still needed to prove it does not apply to me), VAT number, driving licence number, car registration number, cheque number and innumerable others. Yet, before the First World War, you did not even need a passport when you went abroad.

*

I see we are promised a cold winter. That makes me think that probably we shall have one milder than usual. But perhaps the latest pundits will be right after all. They have already shown one startling flash of perception. If, they say, it is colder than usual, then the demand for fuel for heating our homes will be greater also. Amazing what scientists think of. I did not much enjoy the winter of 1962–3, when not a single ray of sunshine was recorded in London throughout February. But I remember one achievement of mine during the winter of 1939–40. I skated on the Cherwell all the way from Magdalen College to the bypass, dismounting or whatever you do with skates at Marston Ferry, now superseded by a bridge, where the ferry-boat had broken a gap in the ice. It was a very rough ride which I shall not attempt to repeat. But I shall walk on Hampstead Heath and there is no more attractive sight than the Heath under snow. Speed the day.

4

I was rebuked the other day for mentioning 'the next war' in the course of a book review. The phrase, I was told, accustomed men to the idea of another war and should therefore not be used. A touch of the ostrich, no doubt, but perhaps something in the criticism all the same. Looking back to the origins of our two world wars, there was in each case an increasing emphasis on the inevitability of war, and as a result the two wars came as no surprise. In much the same way we shall have a good four minutes next time in which to say 'I always knew this would happen' before civilised life comes to an end. I certainly do not want to contribute to this end of the human story. When asked to foretell the future, I answer that an historian is no more qualified than anyone else to make prophecies – perhaps indeed less so, because of our preoccupation with the past. We expect history to repeat itself and usually it does so. In every generation neighbouring states have gone to war with each other. We are often told to learn lessons from history and the most likely lesson to learn just now is that if men behave in the future as they have done in the past there will be a Third World War, more terrible than any that has gone before. But of course the rule is not universal. Sometimes men have behaved differently from the way they did in the past and this can happen again – the joker in destiny's pack. I would not rely much on it. Men used to have hope for the future. Has any sane man now any hope that the future will be better than the past?

*

While on the topic of peace and war, a question comes into my mind: whatever happened to the United Nations Organisation? I distinctly remember that a body of this name was set up at the end of the Second World War. Indeed, I have read a book which shows

15

that the historian Sir Charles Webster created it almost single-handed. Nowadays the mystic symbol UNO is never mentioned. The poor old League of Nations did much better. It settled quite a number of wars, such as a war between Greece and Bulgaria, and the Gran Chaco war, wherever that may be, before it sank beneath the waves. It also, if I remember aright, did something about the white slave traffic, though whether to promote it, regulate it or prevent it is now beyond recall. It continued to hit the headlines almost until it expired, with Prime Ministers, Chancellors and Commissars gathering together for impassioned debate and more obscure intrigues. UNO gives us no such signs of life. If it still exists, which I very much doubt, it must cost the British taxpayer quite a sum of money.

UNO is not the only institution which merits inquiry. I once had a holiday at Monte Carlo at the expense of a body called UNESCO. Is it still around? It once had a monstrous great building in Paris, the rooms of which, with their lavish windows, all faced south and therefore could not be used in summer. I suppose the staff took the summer months off and one year never came back. No one had noticed their curious disappearance until I drew attention to it. There used to be offshoots of UNO in Rome, Geneva, and no doubt elsewhere. I suppose they have all withered by now. If not, I hope their respective staffs have their salaries paid into Swiss numbered accounts.

*

Living in a remote fastness near Parliament Hill, I know little of what goes on in the metropolis. For fresh air and exercise I walk about Hampstead Heath, which might almost be many miles away from London and has Kenwood House into the bargain. Village shops supply most of my needs, though I sometimes venture as far as Kentish Town Road. However, the other day I thought that as a conscientious diarist I ought to find out what goes on in our great capital. Having read about the scandals of sex shops, I decided to visit them. Chaperoned by my wife, I ventured down to Soho and entered one. It was most disappointing. There was no sex on sale at all as I understand the word, only a few customers drifting round silently, as they do in a multiple store. There were a number of objects labelled 'sex aids', but with no indication of how they

16

should be used. They were certainly of no use to me. They did not even make me laugh. The periodicals were even drearier, with crude photographs of cruder bodies. I was also invited to see a blue film. As the description of it was boringly clinical, I thought it, too, would not make me laugh, so I left it out. London sex life has still passed me by. I suppose I ought to visit a brothel. But how do I find one? I can't walk down the allegedly disreputable streets ringing each doorbell. It is useless to ask a taxi-driver. He would only say that he had seen me on television and then want a reading-list for his daughter who is studying history at her comprehensive school. I give up the search. When I go down to London at all it will be to the London Library, where I believe improper books are locked away in the Librarian's room. I wonder whether they are any more interesting than a sex shop?

*

A kind reader sent me a list of centenary anniversaries which I could celebrate during 1981. The first and most famous is the Peasants' Revolt of 1381, the first great emergence of the people in English history. I wonder whether Wat Tyler lived on in folk memory? My special hero, Captain Swing, must certainly have remembered him. In 1581 Queen Elizabeth I knighted Drake, one pirate chief honouring another; 1681 only offers the completion of Wren's Tom Tower in Oxford. Let us hurry on. In 1781 the Clarendon Press was founded, though it celebrated what it claimed to be its 500th birthday some years ago. Two great books were published: Rousseau's *Confessions*, which I have often read, and Kant's *Critique of Pure Reason*, which I have not read and never shall. There was born George Stephenson, pioneer of the railway age that is now passing away before our eyes. The death roll for 1881 is rich in great names. First comes Carlyle, who is now somewhat under a cloud, though I rank his *French Revolution* as the most powerful re-creation ever written. I pass over Benjamin Disraeli, Earl of Beaconsfield; the Tories can keep him for all I care. Dostoevsky is a different matter: one of the world's greatest authors, though I am afraid not often reread by me. The births are also good. Top of the list comes P. G. Wodehouse, incomparable master of English prose, whose books are, I hope, studied in every school. A cool welcome for Kemal Ataturk, though I suppose he

17

invented modern Turkey, and no welcome at all for Ernie Bevin, high among the combatants of the Cold War. I have an allergy to penicillin so I am not sure about Sir Alexander Fleming. The Natural History Museum was opened; it is now on the brink of desecration. Finally, flogging was abolished in the Royal Navy and the British Army, a remarkable achievement, if rather late in the day.

5

The disputes within the Labour Party, I see, are to run on at least until October, so my comments are not all that belated. I have been what is called a rank-and-file member of the Labour Party for just on 60 years. I pay my dues; I cast my vote in national, and sometimes in municipal, elections; I even encourage members of my family to go canvassing. I regard the juggling of figures on how to elect a leader with bored impatience. I can't see what was wrong with the old system of election by the Labour Members of Parliament. We do not want a Leader with a capital letter; this is English for *Duce* or *Führer*. In practice Labour leaders are not elected. They emerge, and this is merely confirmed by their election. On the whole the party has always managed to find the best man available. Would election under the new system have produced MacDonald in 1922 or Attlee in 1935? I doubt it. Yet they were the best leaders Labour has had, despite what happened to Mac-Donald in the end.

As to the arguments over policy, they boil down to a question that has racked the Labour Party since its foundation: is the Labour Party socialist or is it not? Time and again this issue has been fought. Time and again the non-socialist Right has won, only to be shaken by a new movement from the Left. This time there is one vital difference. Previously, when the Left lost, it acquiesced and continued to co-operate with the party. Now, when the Right have apparently lost, they announce that the Labour Party has lost its soul and that they are leaving it as soon as they can find a safe refuge elsewhere. I wish they would clear out and leave us alone. Benn wanted to exact a declaration of loyalty. This is unnecessary. Every genuine member of the Labour Party is loyal already.

This brings me to that curious body, the Council for Social Democracy. It has no right to the name. Historically, social democrat was another name for Marxist and, strictly, still is. Marx himself was a social democrat. So was Lenin. His party was the Russian Social Democratic Party (Bolshevik section) until after the October Revolution. It seems to me that the Council is neither socialist nor democratic.

We are told that the new party, if it ever comes into existence, will triumph at the next general election. This is to fly in the face of history, though even the impossible can happen. But look at the record. The Whigs split over the French Revolution. The majority of them supported Pitt. Fox was left with a remnant of 40. But the Whig Party that carried the Reform Bill and other great measures was the party of Mr Fox, not the party of those who deserted him. What happened to the Liberal Unionists whom Joseph Chamberlain carried off against Gladstone? After defeating Home Rule, with disastrous effects for the future of Ireland, they failed to secure any of their measures and 25 years later the Tories ate them up. What happened to the British Workers' Party, Labour renegades who supported Lloyd George in the general election of 1918? They won some seats in that election and then were lost to sight. There is a closer parallel or even perhaps two. In 1931 a handful of Labour MPs went over with MacDonald and formed the National Labour Party. Where are they now? It is almost too unkind to mention my last example: a man who knew better than the Labour Party how to run the Labour Party. It was called the New Party and its leader was Sir Oswald Mosley.

*

Some public benefactors are honoured in their lifetime. Some pass away almost unnoticed. Such a one was Frank Noble, by profession a WEA tutor and organiser, who died last year at the early age of 54. In his spare time Frank Noble inspired and largely created the Offa's Dyke Path which now runs from Chepstow to Prestatyn, not always strictly along the line of the Dyke. It was Frank who negotiated with landowners and farmers, led teams of WEA students to clear the way, and finally secured recognition for the Dyke Path as a public monument. I have walked most of the Pennine Way, some of the Ridgeway, and stretches of other Ways. But I say without hesitation that Offa's Dyke is the finest of the lot, even if some of it was the invention of Sir Cyril Fox rather than of

20

King Offa. Finest for its combination of nature and history; finest for its remoteness from towns and cities; finest for its switchback character which makes it tougher going than many Ways that rise higher. Of course we all honour Tom Stephenson, pioneer of the Pennine Way, first of the Ways and still the grandest of them. But Offa's Dyke Way is the one I remember and to which I hope most to return. I rejoice therefore to set down this tribute to Frank Noble, its begetter. He did more for the happiness of mankind than many more famous figures. Future generations, if there are any, will bless his name as they walk along the Way that he created.

*

I am fascinated by the storm of controversy that is blowing through the English Faculty in Cambridge. We all remember with pleasure the Leavis storm which disturbed Cambridge for many years. I never understood what it was about, something to do with Dickens and D. H. Lawrence, I believe. As I rate the first among the greatest of English novelists and find Lawrence unreadable except for *Sons and Lovers*, I felt very much on the sidelines. This time it seems to be about the Marxist interpretation of literature. I wonder first of all how the members of the English Faculty know what one of their colleagues teaches. Do they slip into his lectures disguised as cleaners or electricians? None of my colleagues ever listened to me except when I gave the Ford Lectures. Or do they collect reports from his pupils? This would be most unprofessional conduct. Live and let live should be the academic's guiding motto, as it has always been mine. Still more important, what *is* the Marxist interpretation of literature? It is all Greek to me, just like the Marxist interpretation of history. Marx himself might have provided the answer if he had ever written his projected book on Balzac, a novelist who certainly thought capital important. Do verses scan differently in the Marxist interpretation? Is more attention paid to royalties than to literary excellence? Of course, economics dictate to us the length of our books and sometimes even their subject. But I doubt whether they create literary genius. I shall watch further developments of the controversy with admiring curiosity. Meanwhile I propose to read that profound study of the lower middle class, *The Diary of a Nobody*.

21

6

Venice should have given me the first entry in this week's Diary – a little family party over the late Spring Bank Holiday. Fate intervened in the shape of the air controllers, whoever they may be: confusion of airway timetables, chaos at the airports. I always get wry satisfaction from the breakdown of our modern devices: aircraft that fly ever faster and carry more people; air control, so-called, spreading across the skies. Then the forgotten human factor intervenes and the fantastic structure goes wrong so that we should have done better to stick to trains. In my disappointment over our cancelled visit I reflected on the changed character of strikes. Once they were directed against the great and powerful. They hit the boss where it hurt him worst, in his pocket. Now they are directed against the weak and defenceless. No business tycoon is disturbed by trouble at Heathrow: he is safely away in his firm's private jet. The Prime Minister can set off on her continental travels whenever it suits her and I dare say the same is true of lesser politicians. But family excursions over a late spring weekend are reduced to confusion or ruined. Our economy has become a permanent battlefield over the bodies of the feeble and unorganised. 'Women and children first' has been stood on its head: now it means that women and children should be the principal victims of industrial disputes. Pensioners also suffer; serves them right for living for so long. I add the subversive thought that the air controllers might have been less resolute if we had stuck to the traditional Whit weekend. Certainly the weather could not have been worse.

*

Baulked of Venice, I went on holiday in Shropshire, perhaps the most remote of English counties and one which I had not visited

22

extensively for 20 years. We went over the industrial museum at Ironbridge; very instructive, no doubt, but rather overwhelming for me; the best of its products is a home-made pork pie, nearly as good as those made at Skipton. I was once more thwarted in my attempt to visit Langley Chapel. A notice said: 'Key with the custodian at Acton Burnell castle.' Acton Burnell is six miles away. When you get there, you find no custodian at the castle, only a box for voluntary contributions.

Our hotel provided me with a new insight. Most country hotels now cater for coach tours. They strive to be like one another. A feature now spreading across the country is an item on the breakfast menu, 'The grilled breakfast'. This sounds like a traditional dish. It is nothing of the sort. A true mixed grill is something quite different and normally eaten at lunchtime or in the evening. 'The grilled breakfast' is an echo of that staple food, bacon and egg, with sausage, tomato and maybe mushrooms thrown in. No sane man wants such a laden plate. Another universal feature is that pots of marmalade have vanished, to be replaced by cartons with contents too great for one piece of toast and too little for two. The portions of butter wrapped in tin foil have the same fault. And now for the bedroom. Only enough drawers for a single night's stay. And, strangest of all, why are there never, yes, really never, any hooks in hotel bedrooms nowadays, not even in the bathroom? Where can I hang my dressing-gown? Still graver, where can I hang my razor strop? I am told some people use safety or electric razors. I do not and my strop requires a hook.

*

In the end I managed to reach the Continent after all. It has taken me many years to collect all the great churches of Burgundy. I visited Saulieu before the war when it was primarily famous for its three-star restaurant. I saw Tournus actually on 2 September 1939 when I was fleeing home from Switzerland. I had two or three admirable holidays at Vézelay after the war before it became overrun by coach parties. Autun has always escaped me. Yet it is pre-eminent among its peers: the finest tympanum of the lot and the first sculpture signed by its maker, Ghislebertus. Long ago I had abandoned all hope of ever seeing it. Then, at an impulse, we went off: uncomfortable flight to Paris, I am sorry to say, but then

23

five hours in a train that stopped at every station. It was entrancing, a form of French life that I had quite forgotten. What a pleasure to be passing through country undisturbed by the noise and smell of a motorway. Autun was all, and more than all, that I had expected. Our hotel still shows the room where Napoleon spent a night on his return from Elba, complete with Imperial furniture. The cathedral tympanum has a design all its own, without the traditional division between sheep and goats. Despite the coach parties there was a rural charm and, what is more, a restaurant of high quality. What I had not expected was a stretch of Roman wall, much surpassing St Albans. Five days of a France I had forgotten. What remains for me to see in the remaining years of my life? Mistra, I suppose, but it is far away and there is a risk of seeing Hellenic buildings or statues, which bore me. I must have another go at Langley Chapel.

*

Writers traditionally abuse their publishers. Perhaps some publishers deserve it, to judge from the warnings against certain of them which the Society of Authors sends round. I have had a perfect publisher for nearly 40 years. Nowadays, young historians sometimes ask my advice on how to bring out a book. I say the usual things: cut down on commas; insist on having the references at the foot of the page; provide adequate maps. Above all, enlist Hamish Hamilton Ltd as your publishers. The other night I had the opportunity to say thank you. The firm celebrated its 50 years of publishing with a champagne party in the Middle Temple Hall. I, long dismissed as an enfant terrible, had now matured into the firm's senior author and spoke for all my grateful colleagues. Again and again Hamish Hamilton Ltd saved my professional life. Early in my career, PWE,* which sounds like an English version of the KGB but wasn't, rejected a piece of mine on the Weimar Republic. Hamish Hamilton encouraged me to turn it into a book. Its view was much deplored in England but is now the standard version among younger German historians. Then another firm remaindered a book of mine on the Habsburg monarchy and let it fall out of print. Hamish Hamilton took it – it is still selling. Hamish Hamilton persuaded me to write a biography of Bismarck. Indeed

* Political Warfare Executive.

without him I should never have become an historian of Germany at all. Hamish Hamilton found the title, *The Troublemakers*, for my favourite brain-child. Looking back over my life, everything in it seems to have happened by accident. Meeting Hamish Hamilton and being ranked among his authors was the most fortunate accident of the lot. No wonder I ran over with gratitude and emotion. Maybe the champagne had something to do with it.

I gather that after some turmoil *The Times* newspaper has acquired a new proprietor. I even gather that I am supposed to have an opinion about this. On one topic I have. If the new ownership means that there will be no more days, weeks or once even a year without *The Times*, this will be a great improvement. To judge from performance in other industries I suppose it is too much to hope. The back page is now put to better use. I welcome the appearance of the weather forecast there. There is also an excellent item cataloguing the closed 'lanes' on the motorways. This gives me great pleasure as forerunner of the announcement that will surely appear one morning, 'All motorways permanently closed at midnight', to be followed by another that traffic in the West End has come to a halt for ever. That will be after my time. I never read the leaders, so I have no means of knowing whether *The Times* has changed its opinions, political or otherwise. I can safely assume that the editor and his assistants have no more idea what economic remedy to apply than has Mrs Thatcher or Michael Foot – or me for that matter. It seems to me that there are more clever essays than there used to be, so that *The Times* increasingly resembles the *Guardian*. My main concern, after the weather, is to learn who of my contemporaries has died. Here *The Times* obits are as good as ever but I presume that they come from old stock. Perhaps the new-style jokes will creep over into the obit columns. One old habit has persisted. I had a duplicated postcard for *The Times* which read: 'peninsular is an adjective. The noun is peninsula'. One day last week I read under Thames Television: '9.30 *For Schools*: The Gower Peninsular, South Wales'. Oh dear and 'For Schools' too.

*

There are odd bits of information that are obvious enough when you read them and yet come as a surprise. Thus, 'this is the first Socialist government in French history'. Undeniable, unless you try to smuggle in the Paris Commune as a step on the way. France was in her day the most revolutionary of European countries. She was the original home of Socialism and I suppose all the Socialist leaders were French until Marx carried off the primacy. If I were being perverse, I might press the claims of the Emperor Napoleon III, who often described himself as a Socialist. In the early 20th century, Jaurès was certainly the equal of Bebel or perhaps was ahead of him. All the same, Jaurès was never a Minister. Léon Blum came nearest to eminence when he was Premier of a coalition. Indeed, I have a vague recollection that he briefly headed an all-Socialist ministry in 1948, but it was no doubt too brief to count. There is another odd thing about the new French government. Not only is it the first Socialist government; it has been welcomed as a victory for moderation and political common sense. No one anticipates that the streets of Paris will be running with blood. Even more extraordinary, in a period when the economic system called capitalism is clearly approaching collapse, the French Communist Party is also running down so that it is a toss-up whether capitalism or Communism will collapse first. Meanwhile, the Socialist Party, now securely in power, has become the guardian of order and the champion of traditional virtues.

*

Our universities are in trouble. This is the lamentable, though inevitable, consequence of the financial transformation by which they became primarily dependent on the state instead of serving the community from their endowments and the fees of their students. That in its turn was the consequence of the elevation of the sciences to their present primacy. Laboratories and all that goes with them cost far more than libraries and, in my opinion, are productive of less good. Who would not give all the nuclear fission in the world for, say, Gibbon's *Decline and Fall* or Macaulay's *History of England*? Also there are too many universities, the result of the helter-skelter of creating new universities some 20 years ago. And what remedy do our political leaders propose for this situation? It could have been foreseen long ago: an attack on

27

the most vital merit of our university system – security of tenure. University lecturers, once appointed, are safe until they reach 65 or even 70. This is not, as might be supposed, to preserve university teachers in idleness, though a few may in fact be idle. It is to preserve their freedom of thought and writing. Once destroy security of tenure and there will be coterie wars in which a faction will seek to discard any teacher whose views it disapproves of. I know this well. How could I have survived the attacks on my books and my scholarship without the benign protection which Magdalen College never failed to afford me? Yet I don't think I have been an altogether faulty historian. You have to pay a price for everything. Security of tenure is the only price that will bring with it freedom of thought and learning. I surmise we shall not have this freedom much longer.

*

I missed the Memorial Meeting to Peggy Duff a few weeks ago and then paid my tribute to her in the Diary instalment that did not come out. So I repeat my tribute now. Peggy had many activities. For me she was the driving force of the original CND. We on the self-appointed executive committee were an assembly of prima donnas, each with his or her idea for leading a great movement. Peggy reduced our fantasies to some sort of sense. Peggy laid down the schedules for the Aldermaston marches, winning the co-operation of each Chief Constable affected. The big meetings in the provincial cities only went off well when Peggy came along to pull them together. If I had been asked to advise the revived CND, I should have said, 'Send for Peggy Duff'. Now she has gone beyond recall.

While I am in the mood for tributes I add one to Philip Toynbee, who died last week. We had been friends on and off for 40 years. Though latterly we met rarely, our intimacy was at once renewed whenever we met. Politically, Philip had two claims to distinction. He was the only Communist to become President of the Oxford Union. He was also one of the very few who ceased to be a Communist without becoming anti-Communist. I could understand little of his books but I understood one of his remarks. When asked, 'Who governs Britain?' Philip replied, 'The governing *class*, surely.' I wish I had thought of that.

*

I am always on the look-out for new walks and have been surprised by finding one near home. A neat little pamphlet by John Richardson presents *A Camden Town Walk* (Camden History Society, 25p), a two-hour stretch of topography and literary echoes. Dickens turns up in nearly every street. H. G. Wells was almost as mobile. Sickert spent much of his life in Camden Town and is also commemorated by what he used to describe as 'the statue of my father-in-law'. Guess who?* Altogether a rewarding excursion on a quiet Sunday morning or even on a busy weekday.

* Richard Cobden.

8

A foreign visitor asked me the other day why English people are still so interested in the Second World War. I was tempted to reply that it was because the books written about it are so interesting, but this was hardly for me to say. In any case, I am not sure that English interest is especially marked. Soviet policy is still largely shaped by recollections of the Second World War. French interest, to judge from their films, is intense, if only to establish, quite incorrectly, that most Frenchmen were collaborators. English interest is more purely historical, not seeking for culprits or even, nowadays, for heroes. At any rate, I met with a cool reception when I tried to run Montgomery as one. Perhaps 40 years or so is the usual period to keep the memory of a great war alive. The Duke of Wellington held the Waterloo Dinner at Apsley House every year until his death in 1852, after which it quickly faded away. Most people do not have a special event to remember in their lives, except being married or, nowadays, being divorced. A great war affects nearly everybody and gives each of them something to remember: an old boys' reunion on a larger scale. It is only this year that the Boer War veterans ceased to meet and the veterans of the First World War still furnish the Imperial War Museum with their recollections. Rightly or wrongly, wars make for better reading than peace does. The *Iliad* was, I suppose, the first bestseller on record and it is about a war. When I was young I read the novels of G. A. Henty more assiduously than I read anything else and they were all about wars. The next war will be most interesting, though there will probably be no one left to read about it.

*

How right our ancestors were to lay down that summer began only on Midsummer's Day. Certainly we have had little of summer so far. But I have been walking on Hampstead Heath before break-fast. On my way I have observed the line of private cars, stationary and presumably waiting for the effects of some movement far out of sight. A similar prospect can be seen each morning on every main road leading to a city or town in this country. There are heavy fumes, poisonous, I am told, in the air. Occasionally the line jerks forward a few yards and then halts again. Attempts to enter the stationary procession from a side-road provoke interesting reactions. Most drivers close up tight, as though to preserve their monopoly of membership in the Gadarene swine. Occasionally a more charitable driver goes to the opposite extreme and allows some half-dozen intruders to infiltrate, to the accompaniment of hoots from indignant drivers behind him. Women drivers are usually more aggressive than men, perhaps because they are taking children to school and regard this as a meritorious act. The whole performance is a funeral procession of common sense. No more perverse, unsocial means of transport has ever been devised, and the least effective into the bargain. A mass of metal is laboriously transported from one place to another. Then it is abandoned for the day, obstructing pedestrians who are attempting a less selfish method of locomotion. Oddly, the resting-place of these ungainly machines is called a 'park'. Such places are not a bit like the parks of grass and trees that I know.

*

Samuel Butler said that he wrote books in order to have something to read in his old age. I have written or concocted 26 books but I don't think I will start on them yet, except to correct the mistakes which creep in with every new edition – words spelt wrongly, lines misplaced – one of the inevitable burdens in a writer's life. Instead, I have just read Macaulay's *History*, all five volumes of it. I am sometimes hailed as his successor. I only wish I were. In my opinion he was the best narrative historian there has ever been, and I am proud to follow in his footsteps. I know that his consuming interest was in political affairs, which he understood from first-hand experience. Political history is frowned on nowadays except by me. But Macaulay was also the wittiest and most penetrating social historian when he wanted to be. He is one of the few historians who make the reader laugh. Gibbon also has his

31

comic passages, but Gibbon's laughter is intellectual, Macaulay's is pure fun. Macaulay was often carried away by his own advocacy. Churchill alleged that he was a persistent liar, which is to get him all wrong. Macaulay was monstrously unfair to William Penn, though it is easy to see why. He was also dishonest in his dealings with Marlborough, but maybe that is less culpable than hero-worship. Indeed, Macaulay's own hero-worship of William III is more at fault than his denigration of Marlborough. No one else would have ventured on the phrase William the Deliverer. Few historians now sing the praises of the Glorious Revolution. Here, I am on Macaulay's side. For me the Glorious Revolution remains the foundation of our liberty. All the more reason to praise it when the basic principles of parliamentary government are threatened as much from the Left as from the Right. However, this does not help my own problem: where am I to find intellectual and literary pleasure now that I have reached the final magical words, 'a lock of the hair of Mary.'?

*

The Labour Party is certainly a glutton for controversy. Not content with having the leadership and the constitution of the party to argue over, it has now raised the question of honours, always a fertile source of disagreement. Because honours in this country are given in the name of the monarch, there is a curious idea afloat that honours and monarchy necessarily go together. Nothing of the kind. The French Republic still operates a system of honours devised by the Emperor Napoleon. The honours list of the Soviet Union must be the longest in the world. The honours system applied in this country used to be the most sensible in existence: the civil servants received more honours as compensation for receiving less pay than those in comparable private employment. Less cash, more Ks was the motto. Now that civil servants get more in security terms than their private equivalents, the system has lost its sense. But as rewards for voluntary unpaid service to the community honours still have their value and justification. Honours for so-called political service, that is, services to a political party, are a different matter. I think they should be auctioned in return for contributions to party funds, and for this purpose the higher ranks of nobility should be revived. Company chairmen for the Tories and union secretaries for Labour should be the principal recipients. This is far better than paying party expenses from public funds. Those who do not like the honours system have a simple way out: they can refuse any honour when offered one. I used to think I should refuse an honour. Recently I have had second thoughts. I should like a baronetcy, not at all for myself but because, being hereditary, it would exasperate my eldest son after I was dead – a practical joke from beyond the grave.

9

I am just off to Oxford for the annual dinner when Magdalen College celebrates the Restoration of its President and Fellows. When I mention this most people suppose it has something to do with the restoration of the great Tower which I am glad to say is now complete. It has no such connection, nor is it concerned with the Restoration of King Charles II. The dinner marks the return of the President and Fellows whom James II deprived of their positions for refusing to elect a President who was not qualified under the College statutes – and a Roman Catholic into the bargain. The Fellows of the day were fervently loyal to the Stuart dynasty, but not to the extent of breaking their statutes. By their resolute stand they did more than any other men to clear the way for the Glorious Revolution which is the foundation of our political and legal freedom. By so doing they won a place for Magdalen College in every textbook of English history, which is more than can be said for any other college at Oxford or Cambridge. I first attended a Restoration dinner in 1938, its 250th anniversary. I now aspire to attend the 300th anniversary in 1988. I remember in my early days at Magdalen speculating whether I and my colleagues would be as firm against Hitler as our predecessors had been against James II.

Footnote on Magdalen College: There are those who pride themselves on knowing that Magdalen, Oxford, has no 'e' on the end and that Magdalene, Cambridge, has. This is pure whimsy. Until the beginning of the 19th century both colleges used the terminal 'e' and Magdalen, Oxford, dropped it by accident. Perhaps the Fellows of Magdalen, Oxford, were less literate. Query: is this still true?

*

This is not the only celebration in my life. I have just returned from a lunch, attended by all the Taylor cousins with their spouses and children who could be traced. We made up a party of 56, many of whom had never set eyes on one another before. Our progenitor, James Taylor, was born in Heywood, Lancashire, in 1848. I am his senior grandson and hence the head of the family, an eminence I had never thought of until now. Our ages ranged from 75 (mine) to eight or ten, my first cousins twice or three times once removed. I am sorry to say that the younger generation, and even those not so young, smoked before lunch was ended. If I had had a family registry I should have been inclined to strike the mealtime smokers off it. Otherwise it was fascinating to see different versions of the Taylor image over 75 years. Stature varied; hair colour varied. Professional interest varied and so I suspect did political allegiances. Most of my cousins spoke better Lancashire than I did but in the same tone of voice. I wish some stranger could have observed the gathering and detected our common characteristics. I remember talking to my grandfather in his old age – he lived until he was 85. I asked him what had mattered most to him in life. He said coolly, 'I don't know what I've done much but at any rate I've added to t'population.' Looking round the lunch party I reflected that he had, more than he anticipated.

*

My life has not been all family lunches or college dinners. I have also been in luck's way with the autumn programme of the English National Opera at the Coliseum. First I heard *The Seraglio*, which should I think be called *Die Entführung* or, if you insist on English, *The Abduction*. Mozart composed to a German text and there is no justification for giving it an Italian name. I first heard this opera in the open air of the castle at Nuremberg. Very romantic it was and also long ago, long before Hitler's time. I now remember more of it than I do of Hitler. Then an even greater treat: Verdi's *Otello*, in my opinion the greatest of all operas. I have heard it many times since I heard Toscanini conduct it. The ENO put on a splendid performance though, having heard it so often in Italian, I could not understand the words when it was being sung in English. The programme on sale stirred a thought in me, quite irrelevant to the performance. It contained a discussion of what the characters were

35

like and what had happened to them before the opera began. In my opinion the answer is: nothing. The characters were created by Boito, the librettist, and never existed away from this. The same is true of all figures in plays or novels and the discussion of their characters by literary scholars. The characters of real figures are difficult enough, as I know from having written two biographies which were mostly guesswork. Imaginary characters have no independent lives and never existed off the stage or outside the novel. This principle, if accepted, would mean the end of most English faculties at universities.

*

I suppose all academic figures who venture into television are a little bewitched by the bright lights and the intrusive cameras. No doubt I have been, though I try to keep my academic values intact. Robert McKenzie, who died last week, was an outstanding exception. He was the greatest of all television pundits on politics and elections. He was the best partner I ever had in television discussions, with Robert Blake as runner-up. I should have been overwhelmed by the number of television engagements Robert McKenzie accepted without a murmur. Yet he remained a conscientious lecturer and Professor at the London School of Economics – always ready to put himself out for a student or to talk over academic questions with a colleague. McKenzie had one unique experience, now no doubt forgotten. In 1956 Lord Beaverbrook published *Men and Power*, a book about English politics and politicians during the First World War. McKenzie wrote to him with a question. Beaverbrook answered by inviting McKenzie and 12 of his pupils to a discussion. After a lavish dinner, including champagne, Beaverbrook then presided over a seminar that lasted three hours. He never repeated the experience. No doubt Beaverbrook did not forget that McKenzie was a fellow Canadian and so came under his heading of 'a very fine man'. So he was. Bob McKenzie was flawless, both as academic and as television performer. He was also my very dear friend. I shall miss him very much.

*

I suppose I ought to make some remark about the party conferences which have recently afflicted us. I am afraid all three left me cold: the Labour Party in an insoluble tangle of voting statistics; the so-called Social Democrats putting on a poor imitation of a travelling circus; and the Conservatives with a former leader denouncing everything that his successors are doing. I was left with an impression of three motor coaches hurtling along a mountain road with no one in the driver's seat. One might expect a crash round the next corner. But in politics the expected rarely happens. The party coaches may go lurching on. I only wish that the journey to catastrophe were made more interesting. As it is I shall happily read a good book or two until the lights go out.

10

Last weekend was not only the anniversary of the Restoration of the President and Fellows of Magdalen College. It is also something much more recent: the 25th anniversary of the Hungarian uprising, which some call a revolution and some call a counter-revolution. The uprising was a paradoxical affair. Men usually passionately anti-revolutionary, like the American propagandists in Munich, enthused over the 'revolution'. Men of the Left, or some of them, feared a counter-revolution. I was one of these. The uprising may have started with genuine devotion to freedom and democracy. It was captured by the clericals and the former aristocracy. I feared a restoration of the Horthy regime which for some strange reason was greatly admired by so many otherwise enlightened people in the West. And how do things stand now, 25 years afterwards? I can answer best with words written by a detached observer, Neal Ascherson, that thanks to the defeat of the counter-revolution there is now 'a society which, for all its tensions, is juster and more widely prosperous than Hungary ever was before'. In Hungary last weekend the uprising was celebrated even though its defeat laid the foundation for the present civilised society which Hungary has now become. This is a unique outcome: a Communist state moving steadily towards prosperity and toleration.

*

'Fifty, filthy fifty.' This is how Harold Nicolson greeted his 50th birthday. Pushing on further with his biography, which I have just read, I found that his 60th birthday caused him even greater distress. This seemed to me very odd. It had never occurred to me that 50 was the threshold of old age. On the contrary, for me it opened the most successful decade of my life. I wrote my favourite book, my most controversial book and my best book, all of them

perhaps better because I wrote them when I was older. By the time
I was 60 I thought old age would come gradually upon me. Quite
the contrary: I became a commuter and had a secretary for the first
time in my life. I also ascended Pillar starting from Buttermere,
which Wainwright says no fell walker of advanced years should
attempt. At 70, the final age of retirement for academics, I became
a Professor, a title I had hitherto evaded. Now that I have passed 75
I begin to notice that perhaps I really am older than I was, say, 20 or
30 years ago. The other day, having walked up the escalator at
Leicester Square station as I always do, I noticed a distinct trace
that I was short of breath. Now I am on the watch for further
symptoms. I am slightly deaf, but so I have been for years unless I
have my ears syringed. I stumble occasionally, more from careless-
ness than from infirmity. These are trivialities. The greatest problem about old age is the fear that it may go on too long. A
benevolent government should issue all who pass the age of 80, or
even 75, with death pills.

*

When rummaging around recently for centenaries to celebrate, I
forgot that Carlyle died in 1881. Fortunately the National Portrait
Gallery has put on an exhibition of portraits of Carlyle to remind
me. If ever there were a man created to have his portrait painted or
his photograph taken it was Thomas Carlyle. Beginning as a young
man of romantic beauty he went on to resemble an Old Testament
prophet and ended with an air of philosophic resignation. As to
Jane Carlyle, the portraits of her in the exhibition convinced me
that she was a tougher proposition than I had supposed.
Altogether a fascinating couple, as I had reminded myself by
reading Froude's biography of Carlyle, all four volumes. I wonder
what the other visitors to the exhibition thought about Carlyle and
wife. Had they caught some distant echo about the Carlyles'
marriage? More importantly, how many of them had read any
Carlyle? If one of them asked me to recommend one of Carlyle's
books, which should I name? *The French Revolution* is the most
startling work of history ever written, but too violent for contemporary taste. *Past and Present* had a wide readership once, particularly among budding socialists. I fear it has lost its appeal. *Sartor
Resartus* and *Frederick the Great* are both unreadable. Perhaps

Oliver Cromwell will carry Carlyle along with him. An insoluble problem. On second thoughts I come back to *The French Revolution* as a unique work and a great one.

*

Every now and then I go out to dinner at a restaurant. More rarely I go to some hotel, either for pleasure or on a lecture trip. For many years past I have consulted *The Good Food Guide* before I set out. Of recent years I have found myself increasingly reluctant to accept the *Guide*'s recommendation and increasingly remarking to myself, 'Well, I shall certainly not go there.' This has nothing to do with my advancing years. It is simply that, though enjoying a feast once or twice a year, I do not want one every evening. As I go through the *Guide* I find a procession of elaborate dishes: dishes with wine, dishes with cream, unlikely ingredients mixed together. Where can I find tripe and onions? Where can I find steak and kidney pudding? Where, if I stay the night, can I escape that horror, the grilled breakfast? And turning to a different point, I do not want to drink expensive vintage wine, badly cared for, whenever I go out to dinner. There is a somewhat related point which also puzzles me. The recommendations in *The Good Food Guide* are mainly for diners who return home by motorcar. How do they drink these vintage wines, and no doubt some preliminaries, without exceeding the permitted limit? Is there some secret password known only to purchasers of *The Good Food Guide*? Or does the dedicated reader of the *Guide* allow his wife to drive home on condition she abstains from alcohol throughout the evening? I should love to know.

*

I am in a complaining mood this week, and with much justification. My target is the growing, indeed overwhelming, practice of publishers putting notes at the end of the book instead of at the foot of the page. This habit is detestable. Either the reader is for ever turning the pages to and fro or he abandons the notes in despair. We were told that putting the notes at the end would make books cheaper. I have just received a book of 300 pages with 80 pages of notes to follow. The price: £20. I always insist on footnotes for my own books. I use the notes to give references or to add to the text.

Here is an anecdote about footnotes. I was correcting the proofs of my *English History, 1914–1945*. I came to a note summarising Winston Churchill's career. The note was a humdrum catalogue of dates. It was the day of Churchill's funeral. I took my pen and inserted at the end of the note: 'The saviour of his country.' I still regard that as the best sentence in my book however much the new generation of historians think we ought to have fought on the other side.

11

Here is a curious little experience which is also a parable. Emerging from Great Turnstile on my way to Lincoln's Inn Fields, my eye was caught by a large placard which read: ITS ILLEGAL; DONT DO IT: DONT PARK ON THE PAVEMENT. Cheered by this enlightened instruction I bumped into a car parked on the pavement and grazed my shin. A characteristic encounter. The message on the placard was correct. Parking on the pavement is illegal and, what is more, highly inconvenient for the pedestrian, particularly the elderly or infirm. Yet every pavement in every English town or city is obstructed by parked cars and no action is taken against their owners. I go further. Every motorist breaks the law whenever he takes out his car. There are speed limits in all built-up areas. There is even a speed limit on every motorway. How many motorists observe them? Do I? Do you? In 1939 I was fined 40s. (a nostalgic sum) for driving down Headington Hill at 40 miles per hour. This would not happen nowadays. Staid citizens complain that the younger generation show no respect for law and order. Yet these very citizens have set the example which the young now follow.

*

It is not often that I praise the BBC as a bastion of free speech. I do so now without reserve. The Bronowski Lecture that Nicholas Humphrey gave on the nuclear bomb would have been a credit to any society, and especially to the BBC; a further credit that it should have been published in *The Listener*. We never reached such an eminence in the days of the original CND 20 years ago. We had larger audiences in public halls, a form of publicity that has gone out of fashion. The revived CND gets a bigger turnout on its marches, or so it claims. Having once dreamt of success and been disappointed I am still not happy about the future. CND has

42

brought out the crowds and secured good publicity. Twenty years ago we sat round in a circle and pondered what we should do next. We never found an answer. I urged that we should run candidates for Parliament, particularly against Labour candidates who were not unilateralists. I was told that we should not win a single seat and that if we split the Labour vote we should be drummed out of the party. I expect my critics were right. The crowds fell away. The audiences diminished. The Committee of 100 advocated direct action and even tried it. As a result the Campaign folded up for 20 years and is now back where we stuck. Maybe there will be a second, bigger wave of enthusiasm which will make even the recent demonstrations seem puny. Somehow CND must have an impact of more than marches and rallies: either there must be a political effect or direct action on an effective scale. I do not think the nuclear warriors will wait all that long.

*

The prospect of nuclear warfare raises a different problem in my head. We have recently learnt that anti-nuclear bomb shelters, highly scientific in design, are now being constructed in various parts of the country. Their exact whereabouts are rarely known but their existence is not disputed. Who is going to occupy them? Surely we ought to be told, if only that the knowledge might console our last moments. It is claimed that there will be survivors of the nuclear holocaust, crippled no doubt and deformed, but carrying the seed for future crippled generations. Clearly, there-fore, the survivors should be chosen from the finest specimens, physical and intellectual, of British stock. I thought of suggesting the members of the House of Lords as carriers of noble blood. Members of the House of Commons hardly pass this test. Then on principle we should preserve inviolate all those who have landed us in this mess: nuclear physicists, or perhaps all scientists, members of the Foreign Office and the diplomatic services, journalists and pundits who have written articles in justification of the murder bomb, and clergymen who have defended it in the name of the Prince of Peace. I was on the point of including the commanders of our nuclear forces. But this is inconceivable. Immutable tradition prescribes that a captain goes down with his ship. No doubt our nuclear captains will remain out in the open and go down with the good ship Britannia. Or will they be found in the deepest nuclear shelter? I have little doubt as to the answer.

*

Official secrecy has more entertaining aspects. Freedom of information has scored some points lately. Thus we have learnt, after 40 years of official concealment, that P. G. Wodehouse, far from broadcasting as a German apologist, gave broadcasts with a high spirit of independence which did him much credit and were masterpieces of his style as well. There was no conceivable reason why we should not have been given the Secret Service reports on him at the time. Better late than never. There is a more challenging case. Sir Oswald Mosley, founder and leader of the British Union of Fascists, was interned for the first four years of the war. He was interrogated at the time by a distinguished lawyer of liberal spirit. Mosley's son is writing his biography and now wishes to see and to publish the lawyer's report. The request is seconded by Mosley's widow. So far the wall of official secrecy has remained unbroken. I am quite sure that in the dark days of 1940 the internment of anybody and everybody was justified. The danger passed once the Battle of Britain was won. Why was Mosley kept in internment for three more years? Leading Ministers – Churchill, Beaverbrook, Herbert Morrison, with whom the decision rested – all favoured Mosley's release. Did they fear the effect on public opinion, particularly perhaps protests from members of the Labour Party? If the explanation is discreditable, all the more reason that it should be given. Many errors were made in wartime. They have now become part of history and we have the right to know the facts.

*

A pleasant experience of recent years has been to regard the church of St Mary-le-Strand from the bus as one passed down the Strand. St Mary's, it seemed, was in full spate of restoration, expensive no doubt but highly satisfactory. The restoration was fully justified: St Mary's is the finest baroque church in London, or even in England. It recalls some similar church in a back street of Rome. Now there is terrible news. The tower, far from being strengthened by restoration, has had its weaknesses exposed. Its need is grave. Not surprisingly, some of the experts suggest the

44

simple remedy of taking it down. St Mary's impedes the flow of traffic. One genius said that the church 'would be better without the tower'. This reminds me of a play by Brecht, where two doctors dissect an ailing man, exclaiming at each stroke: 'You'll be better without your leg, Mr Smith . . . Better without your arm, Mr Smith', and so to the climax: 'You'll be better without your head, Mr Smith.' I can think of many experts who would be better without their heads. St Mary-le-Strand would emphatically not be better without its tower.

12

November 11. Does anyone now remember that this date once meant Armistice Day 1918, and with it a day of remembrance that was observed all over Europe (except in Soviet Russia) until the outbreak of the Second World War? We still have Remembrance Sunday, a day with some vague connection with 1918 and none chronologically with VE Day, a day no longer mentioned in my pocket diary. But the intensity of remembrance is no longer there.

Much else has been forgotten. A former pupil, now a university lecturer, wrote to me the other day: 'It puzzles me now, given the expectation in the late 1930s of aerial massacres and another Somme, why there wasn't an equivalent of today's anti-war movement.' But there was such a movement on a far larger scale, a movement not merely against one weapon, the nuclear bomb, but against all weapons and all wars. Even the *Daily Express* ran an anti-war exhibition and Lord Beaverbrook called himself a pacifist. We did not march in those years, but the Peace Councils achieved meetings quite as big as CND has done. Right up to the middle of the Thirties, war resistance on a large scale was expected by serious observers, including Cabinet Ministers. The Labour Party at its annual conference endorsed by a considerable majority a general strike against war.

Then, quite suddenly, it all faded away. The pacifist of 1934 became the anti-fascist fighter of 1936. The political situation was reversed: Conservatives became anti-war, and the more right-wing they were the more pacific. Socialists marched now for war, and the more Left the more bellicose. The change was greater here than in any other country. After all, Great Britain was the only Allied country that declared war without waiting to be attacked and went through with it to the end. Something once to be proud of. Now it seems very odd.

*

46

I have recently been immersed in the year 1906, a year of many sensations. The greatest of these politically was, I suppose, the sweeping victory that the Liberal Party achieved in loose alliance with the Labour Party – not that the Labour Party then counted for much. It all looks so modern, perhaps a forecast of the next election, until you ask: what did the Liberals want? What did they stand for? Free trade is obvious, though not very relevant nowadays. So is restoration of constitutional rights to the two South African states defeated in the Boer War. But when you look deeper, the analogies become thin. The Parliament of 1906 with its great Liberal majority gave trade unions immunity from the law. After this remarkable Act, Parliament spent the entire year debating religious education in primary schools and the licensing of public houses. In all the years since state education began, what should be taught has never been debated except on the single question: who is going to pay for the hymn books and what creed shall be learned by heart? Devout Nonconformists went to prison rather than pay rates some part of which might go to a Church of England school. Given that these schools were an essential part of the state system it is puzzling how they could be kept going without being paid for. No one seems to have considered the welfare of the children except that their souls would be in danger if they were taught the wrong religious doctrine. After a year's debate nothing was achieved: the House of Lords amended the whole Bill so savagely that the Commons refused to go on with it. Presumably religious instruction goes on in the same way to the present day. But now no one goes to prison for it.

*

I have always prided myself on my good memory. Now my memory is slipping. It takes me some time to remember a friend's surname, though I usually get it right in the end. But I imagined until now that I was firm in my recollections of dates and events in the past. Now I am alarmed. I had a distinct impression that in 1941 nearly everyone in this country was delighted when Soviet Russia was drawn into the war and that from then on what we hoped for, second only to our own victory, was that Russia should defeat the German armies. Surely we rejoiced at the outcome of Stalingrad and at every Russian victory thereafter. Right until the end of the

47

war, it seemed to me, Soviet Russia and Great Britain were allies despite occasional quarrels, and both countries pursued the same aim: the defeat of Germany. Even then there were indications that the Russians remained suspicious when we provided them with details of German strategy and troop movements. If we found ways of overcoming that suspicion then so much the better.

Now it turns out that my memory misled me. Any act which helped the Russians against the Germans was a betrayal of this country. All the armaments and other supplies sent to Russia at such cost in ships and lives – a betrayal. All the negotiations for an alliance, all the diplomatic missions including Churchill's, a betrayal. In short, our whole policy in the Second World War was a lamentable mistake. Presumably we ought to have been fighting on the other side.

On reflection, I remain sure that my memory was right. I have never had any illusions about Stalin's tyranny and indeed denounced it long before the Second World War, as I continued to do after it. And yet, 40 years after, I rejoice at the defeat of Hitler's Germany and have no doubt that Soviet Russia made the major contribution to this. I suppose this only goes to show how out of date I am.

*

Whenever I compose a diary I ask myself: how did Pepys keep it up for nine years and run the Royal Navy as well? For me the Langham Diary has been almost a full-time job during the weeks I have been committed to it. My main trouble is that, unlike Pepys, nothing ever happens to me. Pepys was a busy civil servant. He was involved at Court. He had rows with his wife and flirted, if not more, with his maidservant. He had plenty to record but it is a wonder that he found time to record it. I have never had Pepys's occupation. I do not administer anything. I am not involved in politics except to bestow a distant blessing on CND. I do not have domestic rows, having learnt that discretion is the better part of valour. I have no maidservant so am free to flirt with my wife. When I lose my temper it is usually with myself and that is hardly worthy of record. So I lie on the sofa, manufacturing events for Diary entries, and that is very exhausting. Here is a final entry to record. When I last wrote the London Diary for the *New States-*

man, Anthony Howard ceased to be editor the week I finished. And now, look what has happened. This is my last week on the Langham Diary and Anthony Howard has just ceased to be editor. I wonder what fateful conjunction will next bring us together.

II

The Romanes Lecture for 1981:
'War in Our Time'

In one way or another I have now been teaching Modern European History for at least fifty years. When I looked back I realised with some embarrassment that most of the time I had been dealing with one war or another, or wars in general. I can't claim any expert knowledge of war: in fact, the nearest I have come to war was in 1940, when I and other members of the Home Guard patrolled round Oxford gas works. We foresaw with a flash of strategical penetration that the entire German parachute force would land on Oxford, if only because Oxford was supposed to be in those days a seat of learning. Why it should concentrate on the gas works I never understood. However, there we were on summer evenings, plodding round the gas works with unloaded rifles, waiting for the enemy who never came. That is the nearest I have been to a military experience. And yet war has dominated my life. The first book I published was about the Austro-Sardinian war of 1848, a war no doubt somewhat obscure to most of you: the last of my books, published in 1976, was a history of the Second World War, so I have kept moving. But I have rarely reflected on the general character of war. I do not propose to do so now: rather, to make some personal comments on how I and other historians have treated the subject.

War is one of the most admired and yet one of the most deplorable activities of human beings: its function is to get your way by killing other people. It is one of the oldest activities of the human race. By the 19th century it had become more formal – one could almost say, more civilised. In the last thirty years of the 19th century Europe hardly experienced war at all. The Victorians and their immediate successors attributed this long peace to the Balance of Power if they were feeling cynical about it, or to the Concert of Europe if they were feeling more high-minded. Europe

53

had peace for so long that people began to take it for granted: maybe that was one of the causes of it ending. It would, however, be entirely wrong to suppose that people did not continue to admire and even to idealise war. The literary enthusiasm for war was at its height and such wars as there were, all outside Europe, received constant attention and applause.

Nineteenth-century England is often presented as the most pacific and sensible of European countries: but some units of the British Army were engaged in war during every year of the reign of Queen Victoria. The British Army was an experienced army: nearly all its generals of 1914 had served in the Boer War. Most of the German generals of 1914 with their high repute and prestigious names had never experienced battle at all: their theories, their strategy had been entirely developed on paper or on the drill ground. This unparalleled period of peace made the shock of war in 1914 all the more shattering. It was universally felt that the First World War, as it came to be called, must have had causes that were both obscure and profound. When I was a young university teacher we ran whole courses on the origins of the First World War and if we could find some new little cause we felt we had arrived in the academic profession.

When I look back again I am very doubtful whether the so-called causes of war before 1914 had much to do with the actual outbreak of war. Take, for instance, the great stress laid on the territorial disputes outside Europe: colonial or imperialist rivalries, as they were called. There certainly were such conflicts. In 1885, there was a conflict between England and Russia over some scrap of territory in Afghanistan and the British Government asked the House of Commons for a vote of war credits – the only such vote asked for between 1864 and 1914. But no war followed. In 1898, Great Britain delivered an ultimatum to France during the Fashoda crisis. No war followed. By 1914 all the colonial disputes had been settled or were on the point of being settled. When the war of 1914 broke out, Great Britain and Germany had drafted agreements partitioning the Portuguese colonies and sharing out the Baghdad railway. As late as 23 July, ten days before the outbreak of war, Lloyd George, Chancellor of the Exchequer, actually said that the two great powers, England and Germany, were drawing closer together in friendship.

54

I very much doubt whether the long-term estrangement between the two countries really counted for much. Though there was some anti-German feeling in England, there was pro-German feeling also, particularly among the more enlightened classes. The war crisis of 1914, in my opinion, grew out of nothing. It was not planned, it had not been foreseen, except in the sense that a crisis could always occur. The actual outbreak of war did not derive from any prolonged policy nor did it centre on any burning issue. The prime cause of the war lay in the precautions that had been taken to ensure that there would be no war. The deterrent dominated strategical planning before 1914. When one great power had threatened war, the other country had climbed down, as in the Bosnian crisis of 1908–09. But if all the powers used the deterrent simultaneously war followed automatically. This is what happened in August 1914. The deterrent did not prevent war: it made war inevitable.

The other factor that led to war in 1914 was the strategical dogma held by all the European general staffs, and shared more modestly by the British general staff, that attack was the only means of defence. By 1914 all the European armies were geared for an immediate offensive and each army was eager to get its blow in first. As with the deterrent, every army, in order to prevent war, had to take the offensive which brought the war on. No offensive achieved a decision. On the contrary, the two decisive victories after the outbreak of war were defensive victories: the Anglo-French victory on the Marne which arrested the German offensive, the German victory at Tannenberg which arrested the Russian offensive. Thereafter, the generals on every side repeatedly tried to achieve the offensive victory which had escaped them in 1914. None succeeded. The Germans who had invented the doctrine of the decisive offensive were more cautious than the Allies in practising it. In 1918 Ludendorff lost patience and launched a great offensive which brought final defeat to the German Army. Indeed, it is hardly too much to say that Ludendorff was the main author of the Allied victories which ended the war in 1918.

The First World War, or, as it was called at the time, the Great War, will long be remembered by posterity. Every town, every village has its war memorial, whereas you will seek in vain for war memorials of the Second World War. All you will find is a few names added as a sort of postscript to the memorials of World War One. The only exception is Russia, where there are no memorials of the First World War and many of the Second.

The First World War commanded, I think, a greater degree of enthusiasm and devotion than did any of the wars later in the 20th century. In this country, three million men volunteered for war before compulsory military service was introduced. In all countries there was passionate patriotism and an intense hostility towards the other side. Germany was presented as a barbaric country, though on the whole the German record was as civilised as those of her enemies. There was universal indignation in England when Germany violated the neutrality of Belgium at the outbreak of war. When Great Britain and France violated the neutrality of Greece two years later, not a mouse squeaked. Again, the German attacks on the civilian British population – the bombardment of Scarborough and Whitby, the bombing raids by Zeppelin or aircraft – were regarded as evidence of German barbarism. Before the end of the war that high-minded figure, Field Marshal Smuts, presided over a committee on strategy which laid down that the most effective method of waging war was the indiscriminate bombardment of civilian population from the air. Already before the end of the First World War Trenchard was hoping to assemble a force of a thousand bombers with which to bomb Berlin. The war came to an end before Trenchard could apply his doctrine, but it later became the foundation policy of the RAF.

The First World War had no purpose, except to defeat the other side. The powers involved had to run around trying to discover what they were fighting for. Fritz Fischer established a deserved reputation by writing a book on German war aims, but these aims, when analysed, simply turn out to be the retention of the Belgian and French territory that the Germans had occupied. They were not war aims formulated before the war despite what Fischer says to the contrary. Again it never occurred to the British Colonial Office before the war that the German colonies were an enviable prize. No sooner had the war started than the Colonial Office laid down the doctrine that as Great Britain had always acquired colonies in previous wars, she must do so in this war. Thereafter she was saddled with a string of German colonies in Africa that she later strove to give away. Even more extraordinary, Great

Britain emerged from the First World War with an empire which stretched from Egypt to Singapore – and which no one had foreseen.

Apart from the expansion of the British Empire, the First World War was a great destroyer of empires: the Ottoman Empire, the Habsburg Monarchy, the Russian Empire of the Romanovs all crumbled under its impact. None of these had been included in the original war aims. The Ottoman Empire had few mourners. The dissolution of the Habsburg Monarchy was widely hailed at the time. Later it was deplored by such differing authorities as Lloyd George, Winston Churchill and Ernest Bevin. The transformation of Russia into a Soviet Empire ranks, I suppose, as the most significant change caused by the First World War. The enthusiasms which the war generated at first faded before the war ended. There was much talk of its being a war to end war. Little was done to achieve this. The League of Nations was set up primarily to please the Americans but as the Americans took no part in the League this aim was not achieved.

The Second World War used to be regarded as a series of aggressive steps, long planned by Hitler. Further research and the decline of wartime legends have changed the picture and the Second World War now appears, in the words of a Swiss historian, as 'one of the most gigantic improvisations in history, far above the usual measure'. Wars that had been expected, such as a prolonged campaign in Flanders and Northern France, did not take place. Instead, there were wars in areas that had not been foreseen. In the early period of the Second World War Hitler surprised everyone including himself by the rate of his success: three weeks to defeat Poland, a fortnight to subdue Norway and a month or so to conquer France. By the end of June 1940 Hitler had a more complete domination of Europe than Napoleon ever had and at a trivial expenditure of men and munitions. Indeed, in the year between June 1940 and June 1941 Europe was united under a single ruler as it had never been before.

There was a sharp contrast between the spirit of the two wars. The idealism and romanticism which marked this country during the early months of the First World War were totally lacking. Instead there was a hard determination to defeat Hitler and Nazi Germany, however long it took. 'Victory at all costs' was not merely a piece of Churchillian rhetoric. It truly expressed the national will. Anyone who lived through the Second World War as an adult must recall that there was then a greater combination of patriotism and social idealism than at any other time of his life. We, the generation who had that feeling, have failed to communicate it to those who came after us. I finished my short history of the Second World War with the words: 'Despite the killing and destruction that accompanied it, the Second World War was a good war.' A younger colleague whom I greatly esteem as a historian wrote to me that a war in which thirty million people were killed could not be called a good war. I think we were both right. The Second World War was an appalling war. The genocide practised by the Germans was wicked and so was the indiscriminate strategical bombing of Germany practised by the British – not only wicked but mistaken into the bargain. Nevertheless there was an inspiration which spread to the conquered peoples. At the end of the Second War we believed that the inspiration would last and that there would be a new world. Our expectations have been disappointed.

Instead of a new world we have had the Cold War, a war that has now lasted nearly forty years. In fact, the origins of the Cold War go back much further, to the early days of the Bolshevik Revolution. In 1918, when the Allies were still wrestling with Germany, they conducted wars of intervention to overthrow the Bolsheviks and continued these wars until 1920. What was left was a suspicion that was dispelled or at any rate weakened only with the assistance of Hitler. Once he was defeated and his empire destroyed, the Cold War was resumed. The other day I was reading a book on British foreign policy derived from the records of the Foreign Office and there were the clerks speculating, as the war drew to a close, which side we should take as an ally afterwards, Germany or Russia. Churchill in one of his wilder moments told Montgomery to allow the Germans when they surrendered to keep their rifles, because we should soon need them for use against the Russians. Yet, after all this talk of Soviet aggression, the territory included in the Soviet Union remains less than that ruled over by Tsar Nicholas II before the Russian Revolution.

As a matter of fact, estrangement between allies is usual after a war. In 1923, for instance, British statesmen denounced Poincaré as the new Napoleon. In 1815, at the Congress of Vienna, Castle-reagh and Metternich made an alliance with Talleyrand, repre-sentative of their former enemy France, against Russia, their former ally who had done most of the fighting against France and had liberated Paris. In 1945, a similar alliance was projected against Soviet Russia, who had liberated Eastern Europe. No one in my opinion can discuss this subject with detachment. The Kremlinologists, the so-called experts on Soviet Russia, are in fact propagandists for a policy of hostility towards Soviet Russia: Soviet historians and political advisers are propagandists the other way round. I was once simple-minded enough to believe that the two sides could be reconciled by reason. At the cultural congress at Wroclaw in 1948 I said that the Cold War was the work of two over-mighty powers, each of them regarding the other with unjus-tified suspicion or, if you like, justified suspicion – it comes to much the same thing. No one took the slightest notice, and it looks as though no one ever will. Each side imagines that it has a moral superiority. The United States and their associates are devoted, however halfheartedly, to the principles of political democracy. The Soviet Union has two terrible characteristics which give great offence to the Western World. One is that there are no capitalists in the Soviet Union, the other that there are no landlords. Do you wonder that there is a Cold War?

Instead of wasting my time and yours in trying to solve the insoluble problem of the Cold War I prefer to discuss the only question that matters about war in our time, and that is the transformation of war which has followed the use of atomic bombs in August 1945.

In my opinion, one of the greatest opportunities in the history of mankind was lost in the last days of 1944, lost probably for good and thus bringing the possibility, I think the likelihood, of doom. In the autumn of 1944, Niels Bohr, the Danish physicist who had led the way in developing nuclear science, urged President Roosevelt that the Russians should be told of the discoveries in nuclear power made by the British and Americans. Roosevelt in his usual way agreed with Bohr and as usual did nothing. Churchill declared that Bohr was a traitor and should be imprisoned. Bohr was not sent to prison but his advice was ignored. The opportunity once lost never came again. The American scientists supposed that

59

they would have the secret for ever. By 1951 Soviet scientists had done quite as well as the Americans and the nuclear arms race has gone on ever since.

When Professor Lindemann, Lord Cherwell, first heard about the development of nuclear weapons, he refused to believe it would be possible. When, however, it was demonstrated at Hiroshima and Nagasaki that they worked, Lord Cherwell expressed a sardonic pleasure at the certainty that now mankind would be destroyed and an even greater pleasure that British hands would play some part in pressing the nuclear button. This was perhaps some consolation for an elderly scientist. It is less consolation, or should be, for scientists of less mature years who have dedicated their lives to preparing the destruction of mankind. I also deplore the historians who, against all past experience, declare that this time the deterrent in the shape of nuclear weapons will preserve peace for ever. The deterrent starts off only as a threat, but the record shows that there comes a time when its reality has to be demonstrated – which can only be done by using it. So it was in August 1914 and so it will be again. So far we have done very well. We have lived under nuclear terror for forty years and are still here. The danger increases every day. Without the abolition of nuclear weapons the fate of mankind is certain.

Can nothing be done to avert this fate? We can expect nothing from the nuclear scientists, the political experts, and, least of all, the statesmen. But for ordinary people there still remain standards of right and wrong. One of these is that no country, no political system, is entitled to employ mass murder in order to maintain itself. We are often told that the renunciation of nuclear weapons by a single country – I hope our country – would expose it to nuclear destruction once it could not retaliate. I believe that the reverse is the truth: if we do not possess nuclear weapons there is no point in destroying us. In any case, is it not morally better to face, perhaps to experience, nuclear obliteration than to inflict this obliteration on others?

These weapons of mass destruction are designed and manufactured by human beings. Politicians and military leaders may initiate the preparations for nuclear warfare but the actual manufacture is in the hands of scientists whose devotion should be to the future of mankind. For that matter, every citizen of a free country has a responsibility to help in ridding the world of nuclear weapons. This will not be easy, but it must be done.

I give you some final words of consolation. When the holocaust comes and destroys us nearly all, have no fear. Shelters to withstand nuclear weapons are already in existence for the members of the Cabinet, for the Chiefs of Staff, for the senior civil servants, and for the outstanding scientists, who have directed the mass slaughter. When the nuclear storm has passed, these superior persons will emerge from their shelters and will be able to contemplate, I hope with satisfaction, the destruction which they have brought on their fellow men.

III

Diary, *The London Review of Books*

1

At first sight, 1982 is not a promising year for anniversaries. Almost the only one is just approaching. The Home Office and the Foreign Office were both founded in 1782 – products of a short-lived Whig ministry. This earth-shaking event is to be celebrated by a series of lectures for each Office. I was invited to give a lecture and was then struck off when I revealed that I do not lecture from a script. Perhaps it was wise to eliminate me. No doubt I should not have been able to resist John Bright's definition of British foreign policy as 'a gigantic system of out-relief for the British aristocracy'. 1882 is even less fertile. All I can discover is that in 1882 Charles Bradlaugh, the atheist, administered the oath to himself in the House of Commons. But try the half-centuries and relief is at hand. On 4 June 1832, the great Reform Bill became law under the name of the Representation of the People Act – quite a misnomer, in fact; only a small minority of the British people possessed the vote even after the Reform Bill. It took just under a century for them to reach something like universal suffrage. Nevertheless, the Reform Bill started the process. To adapt Macaulay's sentence about the Glorious Revolution of 1688, it was because we had the Reform Bill in 1832 that we did not have a revolution in the 20th century. Parliamentary democracy stemmed from the Reform Bill, though this was far from the intention of those who promoted it. Present-day radicals are often impatient with the House of Commons. I think they are wrong: the Constitution is the foundation of our liberties, particularly as constantly reformed. So God bless Lord Grey of the Reform Bill and the Whigs who reluctantly supported him.

To deliver the Romanes Lecture in Oxford is a legendary achievement. At least I thought so until a few months ago when I was invited to deliver one. Why me? Useless to speculate. More urgently, what on earth should I talk about? No original ideas simmered in my head. Hastily I ransacked my record. There I remarked something that had never occurred to me before. For fifty years I had been teaching history and writing books about it. All my books and all my lectures had been implicitly about war: from the Napoleonic Wars to the shadow of final war under which we now live. Surely over this half-century some conclusions had occurred to me. Not, I fear, until this moment. Desperately I sought for some startling generalisations. I have always regarded history as mainly an affair of dates and I wrote down as many dates of wars and battles as I could remember. Time was passing. The dread date of the Romanes Lecture was approaching. I shook all the dates in my head like whitebait in a fish basket and hoped for the best. And thus I found myself standing in the Sheldonian Theatre one February afternoon with a microphone as big as a hand-grenade slung round my neck. My impression is that the Sheldonian Theatre was rather full, but you can never tell the size of an audience when you are staring into it. I found my guidelines all right and very depressing they were. Our 20th-century wars started with faith in the deterrent and are likely to end with it. Those who worship the deterrent get nearer and nearer to using it. One day they will have to use it in order to prove that it exists and by using it will prove that it does not exist. The deterrent does not prevent war: it provokes war. Our present approach to war is not even over something concrete like oil. It is purely a conflict over political doctrines: a heresy hunt.

These conclusions seem to me obvious and have done so ever since I campaigned in the original CND more than twenty years ago. They seemed obvious to my audience in the Sheldonian Theatre, to judge from the volume of applause. Perhaps they were merely applauding a retired campaigner who was delivering his swan song. Perhaps the arguments over nuclear weapons are a dialogue of the deaf. Two formidable figures have recently announced their unshakable faith in nuclear armoury. Professor Michael Howard tells us in the columns of *The Times* that the peace of the world will be imperilled if we relinquish nuclear weapons. Field-Marshal Lord Carver, I hear, is writing a book preaching the same doctrine. These are authorities whom I much respect. It baffles me that two men of such intelligence cannot grasp the simple truth. The threat of nuclear war can be used to maintain the peace fifty times, a hundred times, a thousand times. The danger of their use remains as great as it was at the beginning. On one occasion there will be a slip, a misjudgment of the situation, and human civilisation will be destroyed.

There is some cheer on the other side. E. P. Thompson, leader of CND, has recently delivered his banned BBC lecture, 'Beyond the Cold War',* at Worcester City Guildhall with the approval of the city fathers. Evidently Worcester is a most enlightened city. Thompson is a powerful advocate of CND, now indeed of END, truly convincing. I am not so sure about his remedy. It seems to me unlikely that the mass-destruction lobby will be shaken if the youth of all the world gather in tents at Vienna next August. An unexpected voice may carry more weight. There has just appeared in the *New York Review of Books* an article emphasising the urgency of nuclear disarmament without delay. The writer is none other than George Kennan, the influential American diplomat who launched the policy of 'containment' and with it the Cold War some thirty years ago. If George Kennan has been converted to nuclear disarmament, perhaps something good is astir in the world after all.

The death of Peter Opie on 5 February should not pass without commemoration. He and his wife Iona were our leading authorities on nursery rhymes and nursery lore. *The Oxford Nursery Rhyme Book†* which they assembled has been my constant standby ever since it came out in 1955. With its 800 rhymes and 600 illustrations it gives equal pleasure to the adult reader and the infant listeners. The only problem it creates is – where do we go from here? I usually follow Opie with Lear, who again combines verse with pictures. Great fun for me, though I have a feeling that my audience hasn't much idea what Lear is driving at. The same goes for Belloc's *Cautionary Tales*, which are certainly well received. After all, a small boy being eaten by a lion is always welcome news. But I wonder what the audience make of

---

* The lecture is published by Merlin Press
† The Opies' work is published by Oxford. *The Classic Fairy Tales* was issued in paperback by Paladin in 1980. Also available in paperback are *The Lore and Language of School Children* and *The Puffin Book of Nursery Rhymes.*

That instructive play
The Second Mrs Tanqueray,

or even 'Go out and govern New South Wales'? On a more sophisticated level I commend *The Poet's Tongue*, an anthology which Auden and John Garrett put together nearly fifty years ago. I suppose it has long been out of print. It should be resurrected if only for 'The Everlasting Percy' – in my opinion, the funniest poem in the English language. Ah no, I am wrong: the jokes being all about railways, the poem is now no doubt incomprehensible. Only nursery jokes are eternal. As my second childhood is approaching I had better take refuge with the Opies' *Nursery Rhyme Book*. This is the right moment to express my gratitude to Peter and Iona Opie for the delight they have given me and every other sensible child in the country.

2

As I get older – and I have another birthday coming up – I reflect with detached curiosity on the changes I have seen. The most considerable change has only just occurred to me. When I was young we all believed in Progress and so did a couple of generations before us. We followed the guidance of Dr Coué and chanted in unison: 'Every day in every way I am getting better and better.' Progress was a watertight guarantee that, despite temporary setbacks such as world wars, all would come right in the end. Few people believe that nowadays. Take that incomparable achievement of the 19th century: the railways of this country, the finest method of moving about ever devised. Now they are degenerating fast and we are assured that they will degenerate more: fewer stations, fewer lines, fewer trains. Soon they will come to a halt altogether. Roads are an inadequate substitute. A few years ago the motorways were supposed to be triumphs of engineering. Now they are falling to pieces. The Severn Bridge is rusting. 'Spaghetti Junction' may soon have to be closed altogether. I am enough of a motorist to have learnt that it is safer and quicker to travel off the motorways than on them, but one hard winter, it seems, has brought havoc even to the ordinary roads of the country. It all sounds like the end of the Roman Empire. Destruction as an ideal has taken the place of Progress, as witness such varied activities as the riots at Toxteth and the manufacture of nuclear weapons. When Malcolm Muggeridge and I were young we used to speculate about the end of civilisation. Little did we expect it would come in our lifetimes.

I regard myself as a loyal member of the Labour Party. By this I mean that I usually disagree with what it does. Take the indignation against the cricketers who have gone to play cricket in South Africa. I am totally against apartheid. I have often refused to visit a country where my principles were against its government: Italy under Mussolini, Germany under Hitler, Spain under Franco, Czechoslovakia since 1948. But these were my individual decisions and so it should always be. Who am I, who are the indignant members of the House of Commons, to dictate the morality of others? Plenty of English people go to South Africa and for that matter to wickeder countries in order to make money or merely to enjoy themselves. Why pick on the cricketers and not, say, on the businessmen? If these cricketers are subsequently excluded from English Test teams at the request of other Commonwealth countries, that is perfectly reasonable. But I believe every man is entitled to take his own conscience as his guide. I am against witch-hunts, whether against cricketers who play in South Africa or academics who once provided Soviet agents with a lot of harmless information.

There is another question on which I am out of line, this time in disagreement with my old friend Michael Foot. Five 20th-century prime ministers and one non-premier (Joseph Chamberlain) have statues in the lobby of the House of Commons: Balfour, Asquith, Lloyd George, Churchill and Attlee. The inclusion of Joseph Chamberlain seems rather odd unless it be meritorious to wreck first the Liberal and then the Conservative Party. But let that pass. Now it is proposed to put up a statue of Stanley Baldwin, three times prime minister. What's wrong with that? But Michael says the Labour Party will not support the proposal. The grounds of objection are strange. First Baldwin defeated the General Strike. Actually Churchill had far more to do with the defeat of the General Strike than Baldwin had. Indeed it was Baldwin's conciliatory attitude that ended the strike so peacefully. Then it is said that Baldwin was responsible for large-scale unemployment – nothing like as great as under the most recent Labour government. Baldwin was an appeaser. To the best of my recollection, we in the Labour Party were for appeasement and we condemned Baldwin for spending too much on armaments. Finally Baldwin got rid of Edward VIII. The best day's work Baldwin ever did. Otherwise we should have been saddled with a pro-Nazi monarch. I remember George Lansbury telling me that 'Stanley' was the only friend the Labour Party had on the Tory benches. That's good enough for me.

What is Michael afraid of? Is it that if Baldwin gets his statue Ramsay MacDonald will come next? And what is the Labour Party going to say then? MacDonald – the man who created the Labour Party, who secured its first victory in 1906, the man who made Labour the second party in the state and outmanoeuvred Lloyd George and the Liberals, the man who took a brave line during the First World War. Oh dear, what a nuisance historical legacies are. I fear I should not welcome a statue to MacDonald. But then I was against him at the time, unlike most Labour MPs. Nowadays the Labour Party seems to be united only in opposition to their leader and to each other.

Ramsay MacDonald ought to be the hero of that strangely-named party, the Social Democrats. After all, he led a breakaway from the Labour Party, just like the Social Democrats. National Labour actually had a leader, a party organ and Whips – all unlike the Social Democrats. I don't think our political system works except on a two-party basis: either you are for the Ins or for the Outs, there is or should be no third choice. My former pupil, William Rodgers, has just pronounced on *The Politics of Change.**
I sought guidance from him and found little except that the two established parties have made a fine mess of things, which I knew already. I am curious about the alliance between the Social Democrats and the Liberals. If the Social Democrats agree with the Liberal Party, why do they not join it? If they do not agree, why are they in alliance with it? Rodgers says firmly: 'As a new party, the SDP has a momentum which the Liberal Party lacks.' Hence, he implies, the SDP will run the show after the triumph of the Alliance. If I were a Liberal, I should keep a sharp look-out on my allies.

However, I am very glad not to be involved in politics nowadays. They really are a mystery to me. I remember a time, nine years ago, when all our troubles were attributed to the abrupt rise in the price of oil. Dear oil caused inflation. It caused unemployment. In fact, it has apparently shaped our economic fate to the present day. Now the price of oil goes down and I am told that we are nearer ruin than ever. What is more, oil is to resume its place as the principal source of our energy. Coal and nuclear power will both be priced out of the market. All very bewildering.

*Secker

71

I have just read that a piece of sculpture has been cut to commemorate the victims of Yalta, by which apparently is meant the Soviet citizens whom the British and American authorities repatriated to Soviet Russia at the end of the Second World War. But the question of the Soviet citizens in Western hands was never mentioned at the Yalta Conference. At Yalta the Big Three decided that Germany should be under Four-Power control and should pay large reparations to Soviet Russia. They decided that the eastern frontier of Poland should be that devised by the British Foreign Secretary Lord Curzon in 1920. The question of Poland's western frontier was left to the Peace Conference that never met, but it was assumed to be the River Oder and the Western Neisse. The Provisional Government of Poland was to be reinforced by 'democratic elements' from the West and would then be recognised by the Big Three. There were other clauses, including the Soviet promise to enter the Far Eastern war within three months of Germany's surrender. But nothing, so far as I can see, about the repatriation of Soviet citizens. Those who now run this topic, and that of the murders of Katyn, fail to understand the atmosphere of 1945. The Western powers wanted the total defeat of Germany and were willing to pay the price. The choice was between the Nazi domination of all Europe and the Soviet domination of Eastern Europe. Many people, including especially Soviet and Polish exiles, now think the price for the defeat of Germany was too high. I expect soon to learn that the Holocaust never took place and that Hitler was the champion of Western civilisation. I am of a different opinion and still think the Yalta agreements were a good day's work. No doubt I am old-fashioned.

The legend that President Roosevelt knew all about the Japanese attack on Pearl Harbor before it happened has, I see, surfaced again (*Times*, 8 March). This seems to me unlikely. Even the Japanese Government did not know what Admiral Yamamoto was planning and Yamamoto himself did not know how successful the attack would be. One might as well claim that Churchill sent the battleship *Prince of Wales* and the battle-cruiser *Repulse* out to Singapore so that they should be sunk, as indeed Sir Arthur Harris foretold that they would be. Keynes said, 'All business is a bet,' and so are most things in life from birth to death. Would the rulers of Europe have plunged into war in 1914 if they had foreseen the consequences? Would even Roosevelt have suppressed all news of the coming Japanese attack if he had foreseen that half the American battle-fleet would be destroyed? Great historical events stem more often from mistake than from cynical calculation.

3

Most years I make occasional lecture tours for the Historical Association. This year I thought I had done wisely to plan a trip to the West Country in late March. Nothing could have been more mistaken. There was no benign spring: there was either driving rain or cold winds near to freezing. Apart from an inspection of Plymouth harbour, we never went near the sea, which I am told is the main purpose of such a visit. The foray increased my dislike of motorways if that were possible. Common sense advises journey by train, but then how are my wife and I to stagger along with suitcases? I suppose the answer is to stay at home.

Devon and Cornwall were almost unknown country to me, which is slightly shame-making. Plymouth has an attractive position and a character all its own, provided by centuries of the Navy, which still dominates Plymouth though it has now few ships. Dominant personality is still Lady Astor, with Isaac Foot as runner-up. The television series on Lady Astor is not widely applauded in Plymouth and I, too, do not much like visiting-card television: historical characters dragged in for the sake of their names. Crossing the border into Cornwall is the real thing: different country, different people, though, alas, not different language. Or is the Cornish nationality all a pretence? Truro is a delightful city. Its cathedral is, I think, the best work of 13th-century Gothic architecture built in the 19th century, far better than anything Viollet-le-Duc could do. There is also an admirable County Museum, rich in Cornish gold and tin as sought by the Carthaginians.

Cultural note: there is no demand in Truro for either *The Times* or the *Guardian*. At least, copies of both journals are virtually unobtainable. And what did I lecture about in Plymouth and Truro? I cannot remember and would not tell if I could. At any rate, the audiences liked it and queued for me to sign my books afterwards.

Further cultural note. At this time of year the local hotels are largely occupied by commercial travellers – 'reps', as they are now called – reminiscent of the novels of Balzac. It surely must be a dangerous profession: eating heavy hotel food night after night and year after year. Speaking of food reminds me that the only acceptable form of 'pub grub' is Ploughman's Lunch: an admirable combination of bread, cheese and pickled onions, but offering far too much of all three. No genuine ploughman ever ate a lunch of such quantities. I usually wrap up half my Ploughman's Lunch and take it home for lunch next day.

The end of our tour brought us to Barnstaple, an interesting historic town now being destroyed for the sake of a bypass. Some miles outside Barnstaple down a very muddy lane live my friends Charles and Pamela Gott. Charles and I have been friends for almost sixty years. Indeed, he is almost my only surviving Oxford friend, as distinct from acquaintance. Our mutual affection has remained undimmed since the time when we first met at Oxford and long may it so continue. I was much moved and deeply grateful that such a thing could have happened to me.

I am not so grateful that Thursday, 25 March, was my 76th birthday. I used not to notice Time's Winged Chariot drawing near. Now I notice it at every turn. I get along all right but like a treasured motor-car my body shows signs of rust and the sparking plugs do not always fire in the right order. I learnt from Charles Gott that, like me, he suffers from nominal amnesia – an inability to remember the names of people and places. Maybe nominal amnesia is often a blessing in disguise. Certainly there are some people whose names I would sooner forget. I can also offer some consolation to the sufferer. Nominal amnesia does not last. The missing name comes back suddenly five or ten minutes later, just when you are glad to be without it. Many activities are all right so long as you keep in practice. Always eat heartily and drink too, in moderation – that is, half a bottle of wine every day. Always walk your accustomed distance each day, even if not at your accustomed rate. I notice a slight shortage of breath when going up Parliament Hill but this passes if I go faster. I don't expect to manage Coniston Old Man again but I hope Loughrigg Fell will not be beyond me, and of course Tennyson Down is still easy territory. Though I walk more slowly, I read as fast as ever, which is an essential qualification in my trade.

There are consolations in growing older, principally in the form of recollections. I cannot always remember what happened last week, still less last year, but I am sound on events of up to almost seventy years ago. I can't remember what happened to me in 1912, but I know what happened to me in 1913: I went with my mother to Alassio and had an electric torch, then a great novelty, for my birthday. From here on I reminisce by decades. In 1922 I paid my first visit to Mont St Michel and stayed at the Hotel of Mère Poulard. The beating of omelettes went on ceaselessly – not that I approve of omelettes with their whites stiffened. There was draught cider on the tables – free, of course – and we could run wild over the Mount when the day-trippers had gone away. In 1932 I attended the Salzburg Festival, where the crowds had not yet arrived and the prices had not gone sky high. Afterwards we visited Germany for pleasure – never again. We chased after the altars of Riemenschneider. When I got back to Manchester I announced, 'There is a war coming,' and put off the setting of examination papers as long as I could in the belief or hope that the outbreak of war would make them unnecessary. As a matter of fact, when war came, much later than I had expected, the setting of examination papers continued without interruption. In 1942 I remember all sorts of things, but there is nothing more tedious than wartime anecdotes, so I had better break off. Besides, again like most wartime anecdotes, mine have acquired a fictitious character from having been told so often.

However, there is one recollection from the pre-war years that comes back into my mind. I am quite sure that in the Thirties the Labour Party intended to abolish the House of Lords without delay if it ever came into power, and that this applied to the moderates as well as to the radicals in the Party. When Ramsay MacDonald offered a peerage to R. H. Tawney, greatest of the moderates, Tawney replied: 'What harm have I ever done the Labour Party?' Labour men who accepted peerages were regarded as renegades, unless they did it as Lord Stansgate, Tony Benn's father, did in the call of duty. To go back further, before the First World War even most Liberals wanted to curb the powers of the House of Lords, if not to abolish it altogether. And now where are we? The House of Lords has more influence than it used to have. Labour Life Peers are devoted to the House and prouder of their titles than any earl or marquis of ancient lineage. This may be a desirable outcome, though I do not think so. But it is a bit hard that youngsters who remain faithful to the Labour outlook of fifty years ago and whom Keir Hardie would not have been ashamed to greet as comrades are now hounded from the Labour Party under the invidious name of Trotskyites. Why, the most extreme Militant is no more than a Menshevik, and Trotsky did not like the Mensheviks at all.

The monarchy is a different matter. Republicanism used to be highly respectable. Bradlaugh was a republican. So was Joseph Chamberlain. And, to invoke the sacred name again, so of course was Keir Hardie. My impression is that republicanism went out with the Second World War, when the Left was even more passionately patriotic than the Right. Now I see no reason to stir up trouble over the monarchy when it is a harmless, even a useful political institution. The British monarchy has an honourable record throughout this century of co-operation as much with Labour as with Conservative governments. On the other hand, there is no point in threatening with expulsion Young Socialists anxious to be as republican as their forebears. In my opinion, it ill becomes the Labour Party to persecute heretics and rebels. A Labour Party that aspires to become respectable is a Labour Party doomed to decay.

That is enough about politics, indeed too much. Instead, a warm welcome for a new book by that indefatigable tramper Hunter Davies. This one is *A Walk along the Tracks*,* an exploration of the disused railway lines which have now accumulated to 8,000 miles, with no doubt more to come. Some of these lines have been taken over by enlightened local authorities and turned into agreeable rural walks. Some have merely fallen into decay or been obliterated altogether. Hunter Davies has explored ten of the most attractive, some genuinely on foot, others with the aid of mechanical transport. He throws in a generous measure of railway history, which is now a booming subject. His choices range from a line in North London, which I have walked, to remote lines in Scotland and Cumberland, which I am sorry to see Hunter calls

* Weidenfeld

Cumbria. He has passed over the Ashbourne to Parsley Hay line in Derbyshire, now called the Tissington Trail. Its death throes were characteristic. The local inhabitants and the devoted hikers were promised a bus service to replace the closed line, even to improve on it. The line was duly closed. The buses ran for a year or two. Then they, too, were abolished, and now the area has no public transport at all. Moral: everyone should travel by private car. In transport as in everything else, public enterprise is to be deplored.

I am sorry Michael Howard feels that I have misrepresented him in regard to nuclear weapons (*LRB*, Vol. 4, No 6). I understood that he, as also Lord Carver, were firmly against their 'first strike' use, but believed that they should be retained as 'the ultimate deterrent'. In my opinion, if nuclear weapons for first or last strike are in stock they will 'ultimately' be used. As in the past, the ultimate deterrent will be the cause of war. Michael Howard also complains that my historical opinions are not the same as they were twenty years ago. I should hope not.

4

This country has faced the choice of war or peace on some ten or twelve occasions during my lifetime. I was too young to have an opinion on the outbreak of the First World War, then known as the Great War. Thereafter I assumed I should always be against war even when it was conducted in the name of collective security. I opposed going to war over Manchuria in 1932 and campaigned energetically against going to war over Abyssinia in 1935. I even opposed the sending of British troops to Shanghai in 1927. Then, much to my surprise, I turned round. I did not actually advocate war over the Rhineland in 1936, believing – I still think rightly – that it was a lost cause. But I was very hot on the side of war for Czechoslovakia in 1938 and for Poland in 1939. I applauded the Second World War and still do. Afterwards I swung round again: against the war for Korea in 1951 and very much against the Suez aggression in 1956.

And where does this all leave me when the issue of peace or war comes up again? I must start from first principles or lack of them. One thing is quite clear: we cannot simply abandon people of British stock and allegiance. There is no question here of oppression or exploited natives whose territory was stolen from them. Virtually all the Falklanders are as British as you or me. But there is a difficulty. The Falklanders are now hostages in the hands of a brutal dictatorship. To endanger their lives would defeat the whole purpose of the expedition. They are a great deal more important than the alleged oil rights which lie beneath the ocean: if necessary, I would trade the Falklanders for the oil. They must not become the innocent victims of an incompetent government. I should be very glad to see the Argentine Junta humiliated, but not at the cost of British lives. Our mission is no longer to be the general liberator of mankind.

The patriotic indignation over the Falkland Islands stirs alarming analogies with the uproar which preceded the War of Jenkins' Ear in 1739. Then, too, the offence against a British subject had been committed in South America. Then, too, patriotic resentment overpowered a pacific government. Walpole, the prime minister who had opposed going to war, said resignedly, 'They are ringing their bells now. They will be wringing their hands next year' – a hackneyed quotation but none the less true all the same.

There is nothing more dramatic and more emotive than the departure of a great fleet to distant waters. There was enthusiasm at Kronstadt and St Petersburg in 1904 when the Russian Baltic fleet sailed for the Far East. That fleet ended in disaster at Tsushima. Thucydides has described how the Athenians rushed into an expedition for the conquest of Syracuse – an expedition that brought about the end of Athenian greatness. There is an analogy on the other side. Both world wars of the 20th century began with a victory of the Royal Navy over the Germans at or near the Falkland Islands. Perhaps it will be somewhat the same again. And then what? If the British task force returns victoriously home what is to prevent the Argentinians from invading the islands all over again? Must we turn the Falkland Islands into a new Gibraltar? Like Walpole, I look gloomily into the future. Maybe my gloom is misplaced. I write these entries in my diary over the Easter weekend. By the time they appear in print they may have turned out totally false. Such is the penalty of trying to foretell the future. An historian should have more sense.

I add a couple of footnotes to what I suppose we should call the Falklands Crisis. The first is to do with the Labour Party. In recent years the Labour Party has handled the question of war with great embarrassment and delicacy. Officially it supports Nato. Officially it accepts nuclear weapons. But it does so with reluctance. It would like to see nuclear disarmament and looks longingly at the forbidden fruit of unilateral nuclear disarmament. It passionately opposed the Suez aggression, which was the nearest thing we have had to an 'imperialist' war. Suddenly the Labour Party or the greater part of it has become the champion of Empire. The theme of Labour speeches has been that a Labour government would have handled the Falklands crisis with greater skill and to greater effect. Michael Foot speaks in the tones of Churchill in the Second

World War and of Lloyd George in the First. It is fair to say that these two statesmen have often been numbered among Michael's heroes. Still, I never expected to find myself applauding, though with some anxiety, the dispatch of a naval force to the South Atlantic.

This leads me to my second comment on the Falklands affair. How far do the British people share the indignation of the House of Commons? I have watched with regret the decline of popular interest in the British Commonwealth. Few English people are concerned with Canada or Australia unless they have relatives living there. Then suddenly there is a stir of feeling over the Falkland Islands that would have satisfied the Jingoes of a hundred years ago. What has caused it? Is it resentment against the manifest injustice of the Argentine invasion, a monstrous abuse of power against a tiny group? Or is it, as I incline to think, a concealed preference that British people feel for the Commonwealth and Empire, or, even more simply, a far from concealed dislike that they feel for Europe, particularly in the form of Nato? These are riddles without an answer.

Easter weekend is over and already the international situation has changed more than once. My earlier paragraphs now have only historical interest and not much of that. I will write no more on the so-called crisis. Besides, I am off to Venice on Wednesday, another centre of an empire that has vanished. I did not see Venice until I was over forty – I refused to visit Italy while Mussolini ruled. My first visit was in 1949 and there was an episode where I almost achieved fame. The PEN Club was holding its international gathering there. Passing through the Piazza San Marco, I noticed Wystan Auden and Stephen Spender at a table in the Café Florian. I joined them. While we talked, a photographer approached and took some pictures. One of these appears in innumerable books and articles. It shows Auden and Spender deep in conversation. An elbow obtrudes on to the table. The elbow is me – the nearest I ever got to the literary limelight. Now I know better. Leave literary lions alone.

For me, Venice is not San Marco or the Doges' Palace. It is the back streets and open places, the only city in the world where one can escape motor traffic entirely. I have little interest in the great show churches. I must also confess that I do not much like the paintings of Tintoretto. Or rather I might like them if I could see them. But they have always been dark and are now so dirty as to defy my scrutiny. I prefer Carpaccio. At least I can follow what he is trying to say. After a week or so I grow weary at the absence of grass and long for Parliament Hill Fields. All the same, I have been going to Venice for thirty years. I wonder whether this will be my last visit.

I have become quite interested in the signs of old age. For instance, my grasp is no longer firm. All my life I have used an open or, as it is called, a cut-throat razor. My hand trembles slightly. So far I have managed to steady the razor against my cheek. What am I to do if the degeneration continues? I have no idea how to use a safety razor, let alone how to clean it. I have no faith in an electric razor. Perhaps I should grow a beard. But I am told that growing a beard changes one's personality and I am quite content with my personality as it is.

Then my pipe has begun to taste bitter. I was told that this was the reaction of age against nicotine. So I gave up smoking my pipe. There has been a disappointing sequel. My breathing has not improved, which is not surprising: it was perfectly good already. But my sense of taste, which one is said to lose with smoking, has not come back. In fact, it is worse than ever. I think I shall go back to cigars, which still do not taste bitter.

There are consolations. I can read more as I walk less. Very, very occasionally I am offered a seat in a crowded tube or bus – more often by a young woman than by a young man. The greatest consolation of all is that I do not merely nod off during the daytime as I have always done. I actually enjoy going to bed for the afternoon. I think I'll go to bed now.

5

Sitting in Waterlow Park the other afternoon, I heard a park keeper ask an old lady with a transistor, 'What is happening in the Cup Final?' – to which the old lady replied: 'Which one do you mean – the one at Wembley or the one at the Falklands?' The park keeper returned: 'Wembley of course. We have got to win in the Falklands, we are in the right.' This is, I think, the general reaction when people consider the Falklands affair. Stage one: the Argentine occupation was totally unjustified – this appears to me indisputable. Stage two: therefore we are not only entitled to throw the Argentinians out again, it is our duty to do so. This, too, commands general agreement though it is not beyond argument. I do not believe that we have a duty to remedy every act of injustice, even if it is committed against our own people. At any rate, we arrive at stage three: our victory is not only beyond argument, its consequences can be prolonged indefinitely. This final stage of discussion follows logically on what came before but it seems to me far from inevitable.

I am not qualified to judge the character of military operations. It is generally assumed that the British task force will be entirely successful without grave, still less unacceptable losses. It is generally assumed that the Argentinian forces will be expelled. And then what? I do not see how the Falkland Isles can return to their former condition, idyllic as it was alleged to be. The islands must become a permanent military base with barracks, airfields with runways and hangars, and naval dockyards. There must be all the accompaniments of a considerable fortified city: electricity works, water supplies, shops, cinemas, hospitals, presumably even prisons. No one seems to have contemplated the problems of the future. Can we really maintain for good a first-class base at the other end of the world? And if we can do this, is it worth doing? As the questions pile one on another, the wisest course is to cease these speculations and leave events to decide the future fate of the Falkland Islands. This is what I intend to do for the future, though no doubt I shall not stick to my resolve.

Meanwhile I return to my own recent activities. Here, too, I have lapsed from my resolves. Time and again, as I get older and shakier, I determine not to go wandering any more. Time and again, I find myself in some strange part of the country or, even worse, actually abroad. My peaceful old age turns into the wanderings of an itinerant scholar. So it happened with me in the recent weeks. First, as I foresaw in my last diary entry, I kept my promise to my grandchildren and took them to Venice – three boys and one girl. Originally I meant not to let them out of my sight. Then I realised that they were quite capable of looking after themselves. I told them that they must stick together, which they always did, and that they must come back in time for meals, which they also did. They were soon quicker in finding their way round Venice than I was. They also soon knew exactly what they wanted to do: no churches, no art galleries, no Doges' Palace. At a hall off the Campo Santa Margherita they found a hall stuffed with Space Invader machines. There they spent their hours and their money as well. My mild expostulations were met with the explanation that they had large quantities of Italian change to get rid of. My wife and I went about our own devices. Altogether it was a successful holiday, spoilt only by mobs of hysterical Italian schoolgirls. Why are assemblies of schoolgirls, in England as much as in Italy, so much noiser than assemblies of schoolboys? It is wiser to keep away from both.

Hardly back home than we went off again to Lancaster, where a literary week was in progress. I inaugurated it with a talk on History as Literature, which perhaps gave me some excuse for being there. The hall was so dark that I could not see the audience and, as a result, they could not hear me. This sounds odd but it is true. When I cannot see my audience or alternatively my television camera I tend to drop my voice. Though I have driven through Lancaster many times on my way to the Lake District in the days before the motorway, I had never visited it before. Lancaster is a delightful town, well worth a visit. The Castle, still in use as a prison, stands on a hill and you can look across the valley of the

Lune to Morecambe Bay. Pevsner, 1969 edition, says that the 18th-century Music Room is irredeemably lost. Not at all. Enlightened citizens of Lancaster, stung by Pevsner's reproaches, have restored the Music Room in all its glory. It is again among the finest 18th-century show-pieces of England and *vaut le voyage*, as Michelin says. On the other hand, the Ashton Memorial, erected in Edwardian times and 'the grandest monument in England' (Pevsner again), is really falling into ruin, simply because Lord Ashton, manufacturer of carpets and linoleum, who provided £87,000 for its erection, forgot to provide any funds for its preservation. I suppose that by the time the memorial to his wife was finished Lord Ashton had shifted his benevolence to St Anne's-on-Sea.

After a couple of days we shifted our attention and residence to Prescot, which used to be in south Lancashire and is now in a characterless area called Merseyside. As far as I can understand the geography of modern planners, the 'reforms' of some years ago have made two local authorities grow where one grew before. I was never sure when I was in Prescot, when in Knowsley and when in Kirkby. At any rate, Prescot was my objective. I had never heard of Prescot. It turns out to be one of the most important places in English economic history. Eighteenth-century Prescot was the centre of watch-making, not only in England but in Europe. This was a home industry and enough workshops survived to make a museum when Prescot was ruined by the mass-production of Switzerland and America. Now the museum is well-established, though, of course, like most museums, it will never be complete. To crown the work, I formally opened the museum. I made a speech about the significance of time in modern life, unveiled a plaque with my name on it and joined the civic dignitaries first in a festive lunch and later in a festive tea. Altogether a delightful occasion, an excursion into territory as unknown to me as if it had been Tierra del Fuego. We spent a couple of nights at Rainhill, yet another local authority in the district and famous for the locomotive trials in 1830. There is also a Roman Catholic church without windows which I failed to visit – a serious mistake. South Lancashire is not much like the Lancashire I know. Perhaps it was right to transform it into Merseyside.

A week later I went to Manchester: the real Lancashire that I remember both as boy and man. I went to receive an honorary degree at the University. It was like going home. Fifty-two years ago I arrived at the University as an assistant lecturer and was greeted by the news that as the Professor of Modern History had departed, I should have to do his work as well as my own. I was not, however, to receive his salary as well as mine. Ah well, I taught myself a great deal of history by having to give 96 lectures in a year. I can't say that much of the information I acquired did me much good. The University has so expanded since my day as to be unrecognisable and I lost my way in it so often that I became quite frightened. Central Manchester has been transformed for good and ill. The Market Place where Bonnie Prince Charlie proclaimed his father King James III, and where my grandfather had his office, has gone, as has the office of the *Manchester Guardian*, a newspaper few now remember. Against this, the Town Hall has been cleaned and restored so perfectly that it can take its place among the great Gothic buildings of the world. The city fathers, having an outstanding record for destruction, have repented and Castlefield is to become a conservation area, ranging from the Roman fort to Liverpool Road station, the first passenger station in the world, now glamorously restored. I am also glad to report that Tommy Duck's has preserved the character of old Oxford Street, now otherwise vanished. My nine years in Manchester were among the happiest in my life and I was deeply moved to be honoured by the University. However one should remember what the Duke of Wellington liked about the Order of the Garter – there was no damn merit about it. Much the same no doubt applies to honorary degrees.

Even driving down from Manchester to London was in part a nostalgic trip. I took the Stockport road to Disley, a journey that used to take me twenty minutes and that I often did twice in the day. Now it took twice as long and I wearied on the single journey. My hamlet, Higher Disley, is closely threatened by suburban houses but has not lost its rural character. My little house, Three Gates, is wonderfully unchanged, at any rate from the outside. I gave the house its name. I cultivated its garden; I added a large bedroom. I think the rural council of Higher Disley, if there is one, should give me a blue plaque such as many dimmer people receive in London. As it is, I am content with my memories and the view across the valley to Kinder Scout. One further reflection on the way to London. The motorways, once so heralded, are now unusable. Commercial traffic has ruined them and should be confined to them. The rest of us should return to the roads which were good enough for generations before us; if good enough for the Romans so much the better.

Back home I find a pile of invitations to lecture in the coming academic year. I have reached a clear resolve: I am not going to lecture any more. My first reason is that I have nothing to lecture about. The First and Second World Wars are now exhausted, as much as the Crimean War was in my father's time. I said my last word on them in the Romanes Lecture last February. Secondly, I have suddenly become old. Until I passed the age of 75, I was as brisk as I had been twenty years before. Then age caught up on me. Mind as good as ever, body a failing machine. At any rate, I have finished with long journeys or going out late at night in order to deliver stale thoughts on stale subjects. Besides, I am told my voice can be heard no longer. What a relief to close my engagement book.

6

In the days of my youth I kept a diary – not occasional reflections set down at the instruction of an editor but systematic jottings recording the events of each day. The diary became a slavery. Not a day passed without my sitting down to write in it. I imposed events on myself so that I should have something to write about. Passages were inserted in order to please or sometimes to offend my friends and relations. In fact, there came a time when the diary existed more than I did. When I reached man's estate I ceased to write in my diary and destroyed all the previous volumes. I have never regretted this decision. All that remains of my diary-keeping is a reading-list in which I have recorded the titles of all the books I have read from 1926 to the present day. This comes in useful to remind me of books I had quite forgotten. It also fills me with shame to discover the amount of time I wasted on books not worth reading. But this is a habit that still persists.

And now I am back with a diary: no longer a record of events but a commentary on them. What on earth has happened since I last contributed to this column? That sensation of the year, the Falklands war, has ended with complete victory for British arms and we are left with the problem, by no means an easy one, of what to do with the Falkland Islands now we have recovered them. This is a problem which I do not propose to consider, let alone solve. I only remark that I am now ashamed of the patriotic enthusiasm which the Argentinian aggression provoked in me. Posterity will marvel that there was once such a fuss over such remote and trivial possessions.

The events in the Lebanon I refrain from discussing for a different reason. Years of experience have taught me that one should never venture an opinion, favourable or unfavourable, on events concerned in any way with Israel or the Jews. Any attempt at a detached view opens the way for letters, telegrams, personal expostulations and, above all, telephone calls – what the late Sir Lewis Namier called 'the terror by telephone'. He was himself a skilled operator of this weapon and claimed to have reduced more than one critic of Zionism to a nervous breakdown. The only safe course is never, never, never to have any opinion about the Middle East. This is the course I propose to follow.

Now what am I left with? I blench at the thought of the Party Conferences. They have been particularly farcical this year. I refrain from any comment on the Alliance, which I had thought to be some sort of temperance organisation. It must have changed its name and its nature at the same time. The TUC ran true to form, as did the Labour conference. Both bodies displayed their usual feature of being unable to run their voting system efficiently or even, I suspect, honestly. As long as I can remember, the balloting for the most modest posts has been either chaotic or rigged: it does not matter which, the results are much the same. It is an interesting reflection that the nearer a system gets to democracy the more crooked it becomes. There was another odd feature. The greater the decline in Labour membership the stronger the zest for expulsion of members. One day only two members will be left and one will expel the other. I cannot remember whether I was ever expelled. It is rather discreditable to have escaped it.

I had better return to my own affairs. I have finished my autobiography, or rather, I have stopped writing it. Strictly, I cannot finish it until I am dead and then it will be too late. My autobiography runs from the General Election of 1906 more or less to the present day and the more I work on it the slighter it becomes. I will reveal no more for fear of spoiling the sales which I count on to support me in my last years. But the coming economic disaster will ensure that that does not happen.

I had better think of some more routine activities. I have sunbathed often on Hampstead Heath and less often on Norton Beach, Yarmouth, Isle of Wight. I have read a number of ponderous biographies, some of them very good, and all of which I reviewed favourably. Above all, I have been out of England. This sounds more impressive than it was, but quite impressive all the same. I did not realise at first how far away it was. I had supposed not much further than the Home Counties. Actually, St David's, my objective, is further than Coniston in the Lake District, and the road a good deal harder into the bargain. Indeed, it was further than I should have driven a car in a day at my age. However, we made it without much difficulty.

Wales is taking on the appearance of a foreign country. The road signs and place-names are in a strange language which most of the inhabitants do not understand. The schoolchildren, for instance, do not talk Welsh on their way home, even when their instruction is in Welsh. I did not hear any Welsh in the bars or cafés until the customers noticed a stranger, when they would sometimes play the role of devoted Welsh nationalists. Of course, it is unfair to judge the language situation from St David's, which is in Pembrokeshire – Little England beyond Wales. Or rather, it used to be in Pembrokeshire: Wales has been as much the victim of bureaucratic fiddling with the counties as England has been. I could not even discover whether St David's was in a 'dry' county or not. At any rate, the pubs were all selling liquor on Sundays.

St David's Cathedral has the most perfect situation of any in England and Wales. It is one of the very few not in the centre of a race-track. Imagine a cathedral that is reached by a footpath and not threatened with collapse as a result of the surrounding whirl-pool of traffic. No doubt the local planners are even now preparing a highway to pass the West Door and soon thereafter to encompass the rest of the Cathedral. I can actually remember a time when it was possible to walk without hazard to the South Door of York Minster, though in all honesty I must admit that there was a hazard from bicycles. Even more attractive than St David's Cathedral is the Bishop's Palace, just ruined enough to be romantic and pre-served enough to make sense. I spent much of my time at St David's merely sitting within the Bishop's Palace and admiring its remoteness from the world.

Somehow the return drive to London seemed longer than the drive out. Perhaps this was because I was foolish enough to return mainly by motorway. The motorways are a striking instance of the modern world: hailed as an enlightened advance, they have be-come a curse. On the first warning of a coming motorway, the local inhabitants band together in protest or flee the country. Nothing can stave off their approach. The most experienced motorists seek out routes immune from the motorway curse. Even I, less enterprising nowadays, know how to reach the North of England, either east or west, without using a motorway at all. Such routes are not only quieter and more agreeable: they are faster, or at least they used to be. Now many of them are artificially obstructed so as to force motorists back on the juggernaut tracks.

Next March I shall have been driving a car for 60 years. Once I used to enjoy this. Now I am embarrassed at having taken part in the rush of Gadarene vehicles. However, I am learning wisdom. My next commitment out of London after St David's was to Shrewsbury, and there I went by train. The electrified route is a delight. There ought to be far more of them. Shrewsbury was once a great railway junction. Now it is a modest station half-way along the rural line to Aberystwyth. I fear I shall never complete this journey. There should always be some places that one Yarrows (joke patented by Hesketh Pearson and, I think, Hugh Kingsmill).

Shrewsbury School reminds me that Charles Darwin has again become a centre of controversy. The argument is far above my head and in any case does not stir my passion. On reflection, it seems to me unlikely that an entire system of animal development could be worked out after a single voyage on the *Beagle*. This is too subversive a thought for me to pursue. I am, however, very disappointed that those who are now questioning the Darwinian structure have not resurrected Samuel Butler – the author of *Erewhon*, not of *Hudibras*. Butler devoted much of his life to a futile campaign against Darwin's idea. Darwin was not harassed by this, but Butler felt unjustly treated when Darwin made no reply to his criticism. Inspired by some casual remarks of Bernard Shaw's, I struggled through Butler's polemics. No use. I never grasped the argument. Now I have another chance. Maybe I should do better by reviving Butler's other cause and inquire whether the *Odyssey* was written by a woman.

I have followed Butler's guidance to the Italian Alps and to the Sagra di San Michele. Unfortunately, Butler never wrote about his hunt through Sicily in pursuit of the authoress of the *Odyssey*. I would welcome his guidance if I venture to Sicily, a part of Italy I have hardly visited. Palermo especially I should like to revisit with more time and more patience. Its mosaics are an extraordinary combination of Byzantine civilisation and Norman barbarism. Palermo also displays memories of Garibaldi and the Thousand –

memories fascinating to the historian, though dead to the inhabitants, who are now concerned with the Mafia. I have already recorded my more distant ambitions: Mistra and Ohrid. Mistra I shall never see: I can't go there without going through ancient Greece. But the resurrected frescoes of Ohrid are never far from my mind. Meanwhile I must be contented with achievements nearer home. For instance, I have just visited St Martin's Gardens, Pratt Street, Camden Town for the first time. Charles Dibdin is buried there – an appropriate memory in the year of the Falklands war.*

* Composer of *Tom Bowling*.

7

The public opinion polls telling us which political party will win the next general election are rarely right and I don't much care whether they are right or wrong. The census every ten years of film critics naming the world's ten best films is a different matter and stirs my zest for controversy. The most recent list has just been published and I am glad to report that it contains no film less than 19 years old. The critics are becoming as conservative as I am, though they do not show this with some of the films they have recently recommended. I will not mention any that would have fallen under my ban except to remark that, in my opinion, neither persistent sexual intercourse nor lesbianism is a suitable subject for general exhibition.

The film critics have unanimously hailed *Citizen Kane* as the best film ever made, a verdict they have given over three decades. Well, I suppose the critics are right, though I am not eager to see it again. But then when I consider what has been passed over I am not so sure. Chaplin is not on the list at all – in my opinion, he was the best producer ever. Any of his films from *The Cure* to *The Great Dictator* could go to the head of the list, and I can't think of a single Chaplin film that I would cut out. *The General* makes a welcome appearance but far too low: equal tenth instead of equal third. And where, oh where, is W. C. Fields? I am accustomed to name *Never give a sucker an even break* as the best film ever made except that *It's a gift* is just as good. A world of films without W. C. Fields is no good for me. Then I would cut out all French films and all musicals and substitute *Bad Day at Black Rock*, one of the best American films ever made. It looks to me that most film critics do not rate American films very highly. No doubt they are dismissed as too well made. Once when asked by the BBC to nominate a film for showing I chose *The Mask of Dimitrios*. I was told that no one had

93

heard of it. I replied that that was why I had nominated it. I now formulate a general rule: 'The best films are those no one has heard of.' I name two for a start: *Closely Observed Trains* and *The Lady with the Little Dog*, the latter of which could take the place of *Battleship Potemkin*, which was always very boring.

And here is another poll of more urgent interest. Forty per cent of Church of England clergy support unilateral nuclear disarmament, 49 per cent support what is laughably called the nuclear deterrent and 11 per cent are undecided – blessed followers of St Thomas. The man in the pew is said to support the nuclear deterrent. No figures are given for this assertion. The vocabulary used in discussing nuclear weapons is peculiarly misleading, almost as though the nuclear advocates are ashamed of what they are advocating. The nuclear weapons are deterrents only until they are used. They then become the most hideous instruments ever known to man. They kill indiscriminately the aggressors and the innocent. They pollute the atmosphere so widely as to make our planet uninhabitable. Those who make and those who use nuclear weapons have become like gods: ready to decree the destruction of future generations for the sake of their twaddling little political or moral differences. Heroic patriots say that they are prepared to 'defend' their country with nuclear weapons. Is it defence to condemn millions of people to agonising deaths? The tolerance, let alone the support of nuclear weapons by men and women of high morality bewilders me. They are intoxicated by phrases.

Church of England bishops are getting into a fine tangle over this issue. Some of them are fine old warriors. Others want to combine repudiation of nuclear weapons with military security for their country. I don't think it can be done. If nuclear weapons are wicked they should be repudiated whatever the risk and that's that. To these hesitant advisers I prefer Dr Edward Norman, Dean of Peterhouse, Cambridge. He assures us that the arguments against disarmament are entirely consistent with Christianity. What is more, 'everything in human history pointed to the fact that the Bomb would one day be dropped.' But cheer up – 'the number of people killed in modern nuclear war might be no greater than in the barbarian invasions in the Middle Ages.' I have been hastily looking through the New Testament to find the well-known text: 'Blessed are the nuclear bombs for they shall be dropped.'

I fear Dr Norman is right about his expectations for the future. Some twenty years ago, when I and others launched the first Campaign for Nuclear Disarmament, we were told that if we abandoned the demand for unilateral disarmament multilateral nuclear disarmament would follow. We fell silent, and all that followed was more nuclear weapons than before. In my opinion, the nuclear fanatics have won. The United States and the Soviet Union have enough nuclear bombs to blow up the whole world, civilised and uncivilised – if there is any distinction between them nowadays. Projects for shelters are a waste of time. The only security against the nuclear horror is the death pill. Privileged persons were issued with death pills when the Germans were supposed to be coming in 1940. The time is rapidly approaching when they should be issued to everyone.

I had not intended to be drawn into arguments over the nuclear bomb, a topic on which I ran out of ideas twenty years ago. What I had in mind was to write about Dr Johnson, simply because I had promised myself to read Boswell's Life of Johnson at least once a decade and on checking my reading-list found I had not done so. But how am I to get from nuclear bombs to Samuel Johnson? I am sure Johnson would have found something trenchant, even explosive, to say about this monstrous device, but he was lucky enough to live before it was invented. However, I have found a way. Johnson remarked on one occasion when a group of clergymen were enjoying each other's wit: 'This merriment of parsons is mighty offensive.' I can say with equal truth: 'This advocacy of nuclear bombs by parsons is mighty offensive.' Having said that, I can be done with parsons and get on to Samuel Johnson.

Every now and then someone asks as a sort of parlour game: 'Who do you think is the greatest Englishman?' I have never been at a loss for an answer: 'Samuel Johnson of course.' Many qualities can be educed to justify this assertion. Johnson composed the first great dictionary of the English language. Lives of the Poets is a model of biographies on a small scale and I wish I had the gifts to write something comparable. These writings, though admirable, are irrelevant to his greatness. This was based on his character, on what he did and on what he said. Johnson was profound. He was moral. Above all, he was human. Indeed he carried English human nature to the highest point of which we have knowledge. I often wonder whether he realised that Boswell was composing about him the greatest biography in the English language. I suspect that he never gave it a thought.

They made a wonderful pair. Johnson wise, profound in thought and at the same time highly humorous; Boswell impulsive, flighty in mind, erratic. Johnson called himself 'a clubbable man', but I fear he was sometimes heavy-going. Boswell was always lively in mind and talk. Altogether a great combination. Reading Boswell's biography, I recapture something of the pleasure and excitement with which I first read it some sixty years ago.

Still, I have a qualm. There comes into my mind, not perhaps the greatest Englishman, but certainly the runner-up. This is William Cobbett, the People's Friend. Cobbett was not, like Johnson, a great conversationalist. His conversation must have been pretty boring, being entirely about himself and his achievements, from his political agitation to his introduction into England of maize or, as he called it, Cobbett's corn. He was cantankerous. He did not get on with his political comrades; he did not get on with his printers; he did not get on with his family. All the same, he wrote *Rural Rides*, a book packed with England. He did more than any other single man to promote Parliamentary Reform in England and to inspire popular Radicalism. I would read *Rural Rides* again were it not that Cole's enlarged edition of it is too heavy to read in bed.

Johnson and Cobbett – I wish I could add to the list. A few years ago my television producer suggested I should give six television lectures on My Heroes. I replied that I had no heroes, and with that the project fell to the ground. Now it turns out that I have confessed to two. Where are the other four? John Bright used to be something like a hero for me. Now I am not so sure. He made the finest speeches in English, better even than Burke's. But he was pompous and liked the company of dukes too much. Still, he had better stay on the list. I have three names to add. First, John Frost, Chartist and Mayor of Newport, Monmouth, who led the Chartist rising of 1839, the last battle on English soil. Second, Garibaldi, whom I once described as the most wholly admirable man in modern European history. Incidentally, this year is the centenary of his death. Finally, Niels Bohr, pioneer of nuclear physics. In 1944 Bohr urged Churchill and Roosevelt to share their nuclear secrets with Soviet Russia. Roosevelt said Bohr must be mad; Churchill proposed that he should be sent to prison. What a better world it would be if the supposedly great men had listened to the Danish physicist.

8

The last few months have produced a fine crop of books by or about prime ministers: some are biographies, some are diaries and some collections of letters. I have read so many of these books that I now feel I have been living with prime ministers in a familiar way. Six prime ministers have made their appearance, often bearing with them the promise of further volumes to come. Maybe I have missed some prime ministers from earlier centuries, but then the species was only in the process of evolution. Prime minister Attlee, after reading a life of Walpole, reflected: 'I wonder who really ran the country in those days.' The remark is relevant for later centuries.

Here is my list of prime ministers who have occupied my reading time during the last few months. I started with Palmerston, a biography, first of two volumes, perhaps cheating a little when this volume only gets Palmerston to the Foreign Office, but no matter – it is packed with fascinating information; Gladstone, biography, the massive first volume of two, also yet another volume of his interminable diary, a work I have skipped since its outset; Disraeli, a miscellany of works which I also passed by, Disraeli not being my favourite man – Michael Foot can have him; Asquith, 600 pages of love-letters to a girl not half his age; Churchill, first of two volumes of biography by an American writer, a disquisition on his political philosophy, and a massive collection of documents relating to his career in the years 1936–39 which makes up 1600 pages; lastly, Attlee, biography all in one volume and containing very few documents – whether this last is a merit or a fault I cannot decide. Lloyd George I suppose has been written about quite enough already. If he had appeared in my present list it would have contained most significant prime ministers for the last two centuries.

During my devoted reading of the last few months I have acquired enough material to stimulate reflections without number about prime ministers. For the moment, I limit myself to two. What strikes me most forcibly is not so much the amount written about prime ministers as the amount they wrote themselves. And until recently that meant actually writing with a pen, not dictating to a secretary, still less to a dictaphone. Palmerston did not confine himself to writing letters. He himself wrote most of his dispatches when he was Foreign Secretary and often wrote his state papers when he was prime minister. He also wrote leaders for the newspapers when he had nothing else to do. Palmerston's handwriting was an exquisite work of art, and I often admired its beauty in the distant days when I used to study his foreign policy. Gladstone wrote his diary in his own hand, volume after volume of it. Asquith wrote legibly with some distinction. In the course of three years he wrote over five hundred letters to his girl-friend Venetia Stanley. At the same time he conducted the great affairs of state by private hand-written letters. No wonder political events took so long. The rot set in, I think, with Lloyd George, who did not write a clear script. Not surprisingly his secretary became also his mistress and ultimately his wife. Churchill also depended on secretaries, a whole army of them. Attlee has left little evidence. Sir Lewis Namier was an enthusiastic advocate of graphology and claimed to diagnose the character of prime ministers from their handwriting. I doubt this, but there is plenty of material to experiment with.

The other topic which the biographies of prime ministers provoke is their sex-life, or in more general terms their relations with the other sex. To start with Palmerston, he kept a ledger of his sex achievements, which were prodigious – once or often twice a day. The entry 'Fine Day' meant an outstanding performance, an asterisk a commonplace one. Lady Cowper was his mistress for thirty years and he married her after Lord Cowper's death. This did not prevent his having other affairs, including a more or less permanent mistress in a Piccadilly cottage. Gladstone told his son that he had never been technically unfaithful to his marriage bed. I have no idea what this means. At any rate it did not prevent his spending many evening hours with prostitutes, allegedly to redeem them. Disraeli was a rake when young, and later preferred the company of elderly ladies.

Asquith is the talking-point of the moment. For three years he sought Venetia Stanley's company and wrote her long letters nearly every day. The burning question is: did they or didn't they? The editors of his letters 'are almost certain that Asquith never became Venetia's lover in the physical sense.' I agreed with the editors' judgment until I came across a letter ending: 'You know how I long to . . .' Now what are we to make of that – merely that Asquith wanted to hold Venetia's hand under the carriage-rug? I doubt it. Attlee is the simplest and most straightforward, as he usually was. Mrs Attlee told her daughter: 'Sex problems? Clem and I didn't have any sex problems. Everything was marvellous from the start.' Such a tribute almost makes me forgive Attlee for authorising the making of the British atom bomb without telling Parliament, let alone getting its permission.

Gladstone once said that he had known 11 prime ministers and that seven of them had been adulterers. This gives material for a parlour game: who were the seven? The start is easy: Canning (with Queen Caroline when she was Princess of Wales – unlikely, but George IV thought so); Wellington (too many to count); Earl Grey of the Reform Bill (Duchess of Devonshire); Melbourne (Mrs Norton – disputed); Disraeli (mistress traded to Lord Lyndhurst); Palmerston (too many to count). Who was the seventh? Did Gladstone count himself?

I turn my mind to more prosaic parlour games. With my offspring I began with Beggar my Neighbour, went on to Happy Families and finally arrived at Racing Demon. This last tore the cards to pieces and thus ended the progression. The game for four that I prefer is Fives at Dominoes – a simpler version of the pub game Threes and Fives. Cribbage is also a good game for four, but it is on the monotonous side if played the whole evening: the pegging-boards are the most attractive feature of it. I have often tried bezique, Churchill's favourite game, but could never master it. Picquet is incomparable: full of suspense and surprise, with even an occasional reward for playing more skilfully. I still play it quite often with any participant I can rope in. As a boy I was crazy on Ludo, to the despair of the grown-ups. When I reached the age of discretion I wearied of board games. Monopoly has always seemed to me a social catastrophe. A year ago Brian Taylor, my first cousin once removed, invented a game called Kensington which was beyond me, though I hope it rewarded him. Now I am offered a book of Sandhurst Wargames,* which extends from the Middle Ages to the Second World War. These are games I shall never understand, let alone play. It would be much better for the world if everyone else took the same line.

And now for once I venture some comments on events in the world of politics. I have been a member of the Labour Party for just over sixty years and have observed the many witch-hunts of the past with persistent disagreement. There was only one justified ground for expulsion: a group or party that ran rivals to Labour candidates. This has always kept the Communist Party out of the Labour Party, quite rightly. But with the Militants it is the exact opposite: they are eager to run as Labour candidates and are always the most enthusiastic workers for Labour at general elections. I can think of many members of the Labour Party who were not expelled from the party long after they should have been. For instance, Ramsay MacDonald was not expelled until he had actually become prime minister of the anti-Labour National Government. He would have been out long before if he had tried to lead a coalition of the Left. Just the other day the ponderous machinery of the Labour machine did not catch up with its right wing until they had already defected to the so-called SDP.

Before the leaders of the Labour Party embark on yet another witch-hunt they might consider the witch-hunts of the past and reflect where they led. There was a witch-hunt in 1939 – I cannot remember why – which had the astonishing result that when the war against Germany broke out the Labour politicians who were the most outspoken opponents of Hitler were not members of the Labour Party. A few months later, still in 1939, members were expelled from the Labour Party because they opposed going to war against Soviet Russia for the sake of Finland. Many of those expelled at that time were still outside the Labour Party when Soviet Russia and Great Britain became allies in 1941.

I can think of many other absurd expulsions. For instance, in 1947 some twenty Labour Members were expelled from the party for sending a telegram of good wishes to Nenni, the finest Italian Socialist of his generation. I cannot remember whether there were

* *A Book of Sandhurst Wargames* by Paddy Griffith, Hutchinson.

101

any expulsions over Korea, but I know there was plenty of trouble for those who opposed British entry into the Korean War. And opponents of the Falklands war have not been exactly welcomed in the Labour Party.

It is nonsense to denounce the Militants for being Trotskyites or even Marxists. They have no idea what being a Trotskyite means and no more has any one else. As to Marxism, it used to be an honourable title. William Morris was a Marxist. Hyndman, a founder of the Labour Party, was a Marxist, or so he said. There is perhaps a case for expelling Keynesians from the Labour Party, since Keynesianism is a device, not successful nowadays, for saving capitalism, and Labour is supposed to be a socialist party dedicated to the ending of capitalism. It would be much better to forget about witch-hunts and get on with winning supporters, Militant or otherwise.

9

E. H. Carr died on 3 November last. I am inclined to say that he was the greatest British historian of our age: certainly he was the one I most admired. Ted Carr had a long run, varied enough to provide half a dozen careers for any lesser man. He started with twenty years in the diplomatic service, including membership of the British peace delegation to Paris in 1919. After a few years as a professor at Aberystwyth, he was assistant editor of *The Times* for much of the Second World War, when according to Churchill he turned the paper into a tuppenny edition of the *Daily Worker*. He published his first masterpiece, a life of Bakunin – a book I hailed at the time as a masterpiece – as long ago as 1937; he published Volume 14 of his *History of Soviet Russia* shortly before he died and had already made arrangements for it to be carried further by another hand. It is extraordinary to reflect that he began his great work when he was already over sixty and that the latest volumes show no sign of age, except perhaps that they were clearer and more effective than ever.

Carr had great scholarship, great persistence, and above all an unfailing readiness to change his mind with changing circumstances. His first incursion into the discussion of foreign affairs was *The Twenty Years' Crisis*, a book surveying the twenty years between the two great wars. Hence he argued that the peace settlement of 1919 was out of date and that British policy should now aim to conciliate Germany. This argument much shocked those, including myself, who wished to resist Germany at all costs, and I remember denouncing Carr as a wicked appeaser. I quoted the old accusation against *The Times*, with which Ted was already associated, that its policy was 'to be strong upon the stronger side'.

This mood of Ted's did not last long. On the German invasion of Russia he decided that the Russians were going to win. Thereafter he never wavered from this decision. This was not merely his preference for the winning side. He had never been happy in his preference for Nazi Germany. He had greater sympathy with Soviet Russia, despite the dictatorship and sometimes the terror that went along with it. Carr was never an apologist for Soviet Russia, except in the sense of asserting that it should be accorded the respect due to any great power. For a long time he believed that Socialism would triumph not only in Russia but throughout most of the world. Towards the end of his life this confidence in the future dwindled under the impact of events. His last volume of essays – flatteringly bearing the same title as an earlier book of mine – ended with the words: 'I fear this is a profoundly counter-revolutionary period in the West.'

Carr had strong views on contemporary events but he was much more interested in the writing of history. His lectures entitled *What is history?* are intellectual dynamite, sometimes unrivalled in their wisdom, sometimes in my opinion thoroughly wrong-headed. Carr preached the doctrine that historians should not be interested in the losers, who must go into the dustbin of history. This is what Trotsky said about his Menshevik opponents, and it could also apply to Trotsky himself. I disagreed, yet I cannot think of any argument which might prove Carr wrong. Right or wrong, I venerated him and I am proud to record that Ted Carr and I were bound together by ties of great mutual affection.

A personal footnote. Ted Carr was one of the few Fellows of the British Academy who stood firmly by me during the Blunt affair a couple of years ago.

Death has claimed another considerable historian: Captain Stephen Roskill RN, who died on 4 November. Roskill had an active-service career almost until he reached the age of 50 and started as an historian when lesser mortals think of retirement. In 1949 he became the Official Naval Historian and produced *The War at Sea 1939–1945* in four volumes. Though official in name, it was far from official in character. Roskill fought the censors of the Cabinet Office as resolutely as Sir Charles Webster did when writing his *History of the Strategic Air Offensive*. Roskill went on to write more personal books: three volumes on *Hankey* and as a final production a hilarious life of *Admiral of the Fleet Earl Beatty*. He also launched a sharp attack on Churchill for his excessive interference with the conduct of the Navy. This led to a controversy with the other great Naval authority, Arthur Marder, which was the delight of all observers. Roskill was not content to write voluminous books. Becoming a Fellow of Churchill College somewhat late in the day, he took charge of the archive which he and the college were accumulating and made it among the leading assemblages of documents on contemporary affairs in this country. Roskill was a man of sweet temper. After the peacefulness of Naval life he was at first surprised and a little bewildered by the savagery of the academic world into which he had strayed. However, he soon learnt how to defend himself. He had no enemies in the academic world and many friends, including pre-eminently Arthur Marder.

I have just begun on a treat that comes round only once every five – or is it once every ten? – years. At any rate, I heard Brendel play all the sonatas of Beethoven some years ago and now I am in process of hearing him do it again. I can only describe my reaction as one of uninstructed delight. I cannot read a score. I cannot follow a fugue or say with any confidence that a work is in sonata form. Indeed, I know nothing of music except being able to play the major and minor diatonic scales more or less accurately. What good that does me I have never understood. My musical education started quite abruptly when I went to Vienna in 1928 and attended concerts at least once a week during the two years I was there. Thereafter I went to the Hallé concerts during my ten years in Manchester.

Since the war my interest in orchestral concerts has steadily declined and my interest in chamber music steadily increased. My vague impression is that before the war there were a few outstanding string quartets better than almost any around now, but that there are now more quartets of reasonably high quality. As to pianists, there used to be more of flamboyant greatness, including Horowitz, allegedly the greatest pianist of all time, and Rosenthal, who had been Liszt's pupil. I doubt whether there is anyone of that level nowadays, not even Horowitz in his old age. Chamber music has brought me great pleasure during the last thirty years. If I were to express special gratitude it would be to the Beaux Arts Trio and to Brendel, who is now playing Beethoven's sonatas with such freshness that it would seem he had only just discovered them. I hope I shall still be here when he plays them next time round.

My pursuit of public entertainment goes in waves. First I try to find something of merit, devotedly attending plays and films. The plays become more and more trivial; the films more and more offensive. There follow some years when I go to no entertainments at all, except of course revivals. I almost reach the point of believing that all entertainments are unendurable. Then *A Woman of Paris* or *When we are married* (both seen recently) restores my hopes and I renew my visits to theatre or cinema. Eventually I find a contemporary piece of some merit. *On Golden Pond* put me in a good temper for the cinema, perhaps because the combined age of the two principal players must have been over one hundred and fifty years. Here is a report on my recent visits to cinema and theatre.

I began with *Body Heat*. That was a great mistake. I could not understand what was happening and was no wiser when it was revealed at the end that there were two more or less identical girls, not one girl. Why and wherefore was beyond me. The only merit of the film was that though there was much sexual intercourse, it was at any rate normal intercourse – that is to say, bisexual. This is more than could be said for the next film I saw, claimed to be a greater masterpiece than either *Citizen Kane* or *Battleship Potemkin*. This masterpiece was a Hungarian film entitled *Another Way*. It was about a girl with lesbian tastes who sought to convert other girls to her way of life, in one case successfully. Some years ago I decided to visit a show of sex films in Soho. I paid for two hours, but the show was so disgusting that I had to leave within ten minutes. *Another Way* was far worse in its presentation of lesbian intimacy. Characteristic fragment of dubbed dialogue: Intelligence agent (not very intelligent): 'Tell me what exactly do you do?' Lesbian girl 'Sometimes we use one finger, sometimes two, sometimes three.' She ends by straying across into a forbidden zone when she is shot by a frontier guard. Before this I had tried *Reds*, a film allegedly about John Reed. This film had only normal intercourse. It also had a good deal of political nonsense and little hint that Reed wrote the finest account there is of the Bolshevik revolution. I have been cured of film-going for a long time.

I have not done much better with the theatre. I tried *Another Country*, which in fact is a fancy portrait of an English public school in the Thirties. The portrait did not resemble any public school that

106

I remember: indeed, it did not resemble anything in real life. The one merit of the theatre is that it has more and better revivals than the cinema. Recently I have seen that most instructive play, *The Second Mrs Tanqueray* and *When we are married*. I have also seen some Shaw revivals. Every time I see one I am reminded that Shaw with all his faults is the best playwright since Shakespeare, if not a better one. Clearly the theatre has some merits. But the cinema . . .

10

I am just returning to normal life after some weeks in Hungary. Not that life in Hungary is abnormal. Indeed, when asked what conditions in Hungary are like I always reply: 'Much as in England.' I was told that there was less unemployment. On the other hand, prices have recently gone up more. But, in general, life in Hungary is much as in any West European country. One English visitor gave me a fearsome account of the Russian occupation, which he assured me was still at full strength. I can only report that during my visit I did not see a single Russian soldier and never met anyone who knew whether there were still any in Hungary. Certainly the American presence is more flagrant in England than the Russian presence is in Hungary. As to the Hungarians, they are more frightened of American nuclear missiles than of the Russian Army.

In the years after the war Hungary had a Communist revolution. Now Hungary is returning to her ancient ways. Heavy industry and the like are, of course, still nationalised. But what is called 'the private sector' is booming too. It reminded me of NEP in the early days of Soviet Russia. For that matter, conditions are much like those in England. There are plenty of well-do-do people, though maybe living a little more modestly. The main streets are as congested during the rush hours as they are in London. The suburban roads are lined with parked cars at night. The only difference from England is that nearly all the cars are on the small side – say, Escort-type. As I drive a Fiesta, I applaud the common sense of the Hungarians.

Hungary still has all the marks of a proud traditional state. It has an uninterrupted history for almost a thousand years. The actual date of foundation is 896, and since then the Hungarian state has always maintained some sort of existence. The Hungarian Parliament claims to be older than the English Parliament, a topic on which I do not judge. However, there can be no doubt that the Crown of St Stephen, now happily restored to Hungary, is the oldest regalia in Europe. It has a steady stream of Hungarian visitors. No state in Eastern Europe and few in Western Europe has a continuous history to compare with the Hungarian. The treatment of historians and other scholars fills me with envy. The Institute of Historical Research in Budapest has extensive quarters on Castle Hill and over sixty paid researchers on its staff. The comparable English Institute in London has modest quarters in the Senate House and no paid researchers. The Hungarian Academy has a palace all to itself just across from the Parliament House: colonnaded entrance and marble staircase. The Academy also owns country cottages on Lake Balaton and in the mountains, which members of the Academy can use for free during the summer. The British Academy occupies a few rooms in Burlington House and possesses no country cottages. Despite this, the Hungarian academics do not know how well off they are. At any rate, most of them seemed to be away on sabbatical visits to England, the United States or Finland, the latter Hungary's only linguistic relative.

We had a lavish dinner on Christmas Eve with my stepsons and a lavish lunch on Christmas Day with my step-in-laws. We had more feasting on New Year's Eve. There was a Christmas tree in every house or flat we visited, duly illuminated with coloured lights. The luxury hotels by the Danube are alleged to be for foreigners. I never heard anything except Hungarian spoken in them – perhaps Hungarian émigrés returned from the United States for Christmas, but I doubt it. I put on half a stone while I was in Hungary, all from eating too much. Now I am having difficulty taking the half-stone off again.

The Hungarian have one outstanding grievance: the Hungarian minority in Rumania is treated abominably. No love here between one Communist state and another. I estimate that the Rumanian attitude towards its Hungarians is now the worst national scandal in Europe: far worse than, for instance, the Spanish treatment of the Basques. On a lesser scale, one Hungarian acquaintance complained of rough behaviour in the streets. He said people in London behaved more elegantly. I answered that he could not have been in London for a long time. All I know is that in Budapest I was always offered a seat if the bus or tram were crowded. In London I can never get to a seat in time – a young boy or girl always gets in ahead of me.

Now I am back in England and what do I find? The affair of the Falkland Islands is again running in full spate. The Franks Committee had completed its investigations before I returned. It seemed to be high farce. These elderly gentlemen discovered what anyone could have told them: that the intelligence services did not give any precise warning until it was too late. What else could they have done? It had been clear to any intelligent observer (which means something quite different from being in the intelligence services) that Argentina would break out sooner or later. The rulers of the Argentine are in a rickety state. As so often happens, they think that they can capture a bagful of prestige by turning the Falklands into the Malvinas, and they have nothing better to do than play around with the subject. What happened last year now lies in the past. It is a waste of time debating what the British Government did then. The more troublesome question is what it should do now. The Argentines are once again making threatening noises, as they could be expected to do. This costs them little; they have nothing better to do; and they can keep it up until British resources are committed elsewhere.

Apparently it has only just occurred to the British Government that the Argentines would have a second go and repeat this indefinitely. Is the answer for the British Government to enter an arms race which can go on for years? It seems so. This should be an opportunity for the Opposition to offer a sensible alternative – which involves a readiness to negotiate and, in the end, to give way. I must confess that last year I was at first totally wrong like almost everyone else. I went on record that we must defend the rights and freedom of the Falklanders, with the implication that this must go on for ever. Now we are committed to Fortress Falkland to the end of time. Sooner or later this folly must be ended, but who is there left to say so? Michael Foot was as bellicose as Mrs Thatcher, and most of the Labour MPs followed his line.

With deep grief I now set down my conviction that Michael Foot was wrong last year when I applauded him and is still wrong now that I don't. Michael is my dear friend, as he has been for many years past. This will not be the first occasion for him to complain that I have stabbed him in the back. Now I do it with good reason. The Anglo-Argentinian dispute over the Falkland Islands must never again be allowed to turn into war. This can be secured only by concessions, indeed ultimately by surrender, on the British side. Those who advocate this will no doubt become unpopular, but they will be right all the same. Michael cannot take this line: he is too committed to reliance on force already. The only man who has shown common sense from the beginning is Tony Benn. He still shows it every time he speaks, and in my opinion is now the only man fit to lead the Labour Party if that party wants to free itself from the taint of imperialism and sabre-rattling.

One small disadvantage of living in Hungary was that I was often too lazy to climb Castle Hill, and so missed buying *The Times* at the Hilton Hotel. Occasionally when I did climb up I was told, whether correctly I do not know, that *The Times* was on strike. At any rate, I missed the obits for some weeks. Since returning home, I have done laborious research on *The Times* in the London Library. The name that stirred my memories and regrets most was Canon John Collins, who died on New Year's Eve. John Collins was that very rare thing: a good man. He was not particularly a rebel or a radical. He was very conventional in many of his ways, as in being a Canon of St Paul's. But once he saw the right thing to do, nothing could deter him from doing it. For many years he was the outstanding champion in Great Britain of coloured people all over the world. His activity was always practical: fund-raising, legal advocacy and so on. More than anyone else, he was the founder of CND, first phase, and he kept CND on the right lines for years. In the early days of CND he and I toured as a duo: John took the chair and pleaded – most effectively – for money; I started with hard reasoning which usually turned into rabble-rousing. I have never enjoyed myself more than when John and I took Glasgow or some other great city by storm. I agreed with almost everything that John said and did, particularly when the extremists of CND got out of hand. John never quarrelled with CND, but I think he was happy to get back to the coloured peoples.

I have never before commented on an article in a previous number of the *London Review of Books*. I cannot hold back from doing so now. In my opinion, Norman Stone's article on E. H. Carr was wrong at almost every point. I am not well enough versed in Russian and Soviet history to judge how much justice there is in Stone's criticism of Carr's major work – I should guess a good deal. But Carr can also show a shelfful of masterpieces – from *Michael Bakunin* and the *Twenty Years' Crisis* to *What is history?* or his last volume of essays. Stone is totally wrong on Carr as a personality. Carr could be an enchanting companion and at the same time a ruthless critic. He went very much his own way. Very often he had to because of the persecution he endured from more respectable circles. I will not now reveal the name of the Oxford college where he was refused a fellowship solely because his marriage had been dissolved. Instead I will repeat what I have said here before: that Ted Carr was one of the very few Fellows of the British Academy who stood by me in the Blunt affair. He said to me: 'Why do you do it – always making trouble?' But he stood by me all the same.

11

These are troubled times. We have a strike of water workers. I have been worrying for weeks whether the water would continue to run out of the taps. I even laid in a stock of Perrier water. In London at any rate, the water still runs. As to the Perrier water, almost my favourite drink, I cannot allow myself to drink it until the situation becomes acute. Then there are the interminable talks over the limitations or even reduction of nuclear weapons. The outcome of these talks is easy to surmise: they will end with all the nuclear powers possessing more nuclear weapons than they did when the talks started. Once I would have worried about this also. Now I look forward to drinking the Perrier water even if the water talks succeed.

To speak the truth, not an invariable practice with me, I do not care in the slightest about the nuclear talks and their outcome, I do not even care very much whether water will run out of the taps. Something far graver weighs upon me day and night: my wife is in hospital.

She is not gravely ill, though the doctors have not yet found out what is the matter with her. In a few weeks' time, perhaps in a few days, she will be returned to me fit and well. This is no consolation for the devastation my wife's absence causes me. My problems begin early. As soon as I am dressed I have to make the bed and it is no joke making a double bed single-handed. I have to run from one side of the bed to the other and no sooner is one side smoothly tucked in than the other side gets out of order again. Making a single bed is easy; the problem of tackling the double bed alone is one I have never had to face before.

Then there is the problem of getting dressed. I can get dressed all right but normally I rely on my wife to tell me whether I have done it correctly. Now I can only rely on the mirror, which is pretty useless when I am trying to tie a bow tie – I think I am one of the few men in England who wears one on alternate days. Breakfast is the only safe time in the day: I have been making breakfast, whether for a large family or none at all, for the last fifty years. My routine has never varied: bacon and egg, bacon and mushroom, kipper, and so round again. Washing-up is rather a problem. I have always held that as the one who makes the breakfast I am automatically exempt from taking any share in the washing-up. Now my wife is not here, and if I do not wash up, the dirty dishes will still be there when I begin to make dinner in the evening.

The most acute problem for the solitary housekeeper is the shopping. For years past I have relied on my wife either to do the shopping or to give me a list of what I should buy. Now I have to make the list and nothing comes into my head. I check every single item to see whether we have any left. I make a list. On my way to the shops the idea comes into my head of things I might have forgotten. So I go back home to see whether there is a perfectly adequate supply already. When I finally reach the grocer's shop I wander desolately up and down the aisles of shelves seeking what I wished to purchase. My search is usually in vain. In my younger days when I used to go shopping a courteous grocer took my order without any of this search, and the goods I ordered were delivered the same afternoon. Now I have to pull my trolley laboriously homeward. Civilisation is certainly breaking down – indeed, has already done so.

Cooking a solitary dinner is the worst of all. I understand the rudiments of cooking. You place the object to be cooked in a pan, light the gas under the pan and the rest answers for itself. But how long does the object take to be cooked? Apparently the objects vary one from another. I am told I should use the oven for some objects but I cannot find out how to light the oven, so I have given up that idea.

Well, that is enough of my domestic troubles. I turn to a more cheerful subject. During my solitary evenings I have been reading the two volumes of Thomas Hardy's biography by Robert Gittings. I have just finished it and this recalls to me Hardy's funeral at Westminster Abbey, which I actually attended. Or rather the funeral of most of him: his heart had been left behind in Dorsetshire. I suppose I was one of the 'gate-crashers' of whom Mr

Gittings writes so disapprovingly. I entered by the north transept door merely by showing my visiting-card and was ushered into a choir stall just where the coffin came to a halt. The pall-bearers or chief mourners were an odd assembly. First came the Prime Minister, Stanley Baldwin, and the Leader of the Opposition, Ramsay MacDonald. Baldwin had some idea what to do at an Anglican service: MacDonald was much at sea and missed some of his cues. Then came John Galsworthy and Bernard Shaw, presumably the literary kings of the time. Galsworthy behaved impeccably, doing everything absolutely right. Shaw got enjoyment by looking around most of the time. The next pair were Edmund Gosse and J. M. Barrie. Barrie had arranged the whole thing, so I suppose he was entitled to be there. Gosse had been a friend of Hardy's in earlier days, so there was an excuse for his presence too. But why Kipling and Housman had been chosen to wind up the procession is beyond me. Perhaps they were rewarded for literary merit. Altogether an old-fashioned conspectus of the Dean's literary taste. The rearguard was composed of the Vice-Chancellors of Oxford and Cambridge Universities, singular mourners of Jude's creator. The funeral was in January 1928. It now occurs to me that I may be the last survivor of those who attended it. At any rate I am the only one who has set down his impressions of this macabre occasion.

Hitler became German Chancellor just over fifty years ago, on 30 January 1933. Nearly every historian-journalist has had a go at the subject. I certainly did with 1200 words in the *New York Times*. Revisiting these distant years, I found, as I ought to have remembered, that the subject was not very interesting. There was no seizure of power, only Hitler's elevation in a strictly constitutional way. Of course Hitler soon changed all that and began a procedure which led him to dictatorship, though this took him longer than is often supposed. Hitler's first step to his breach with legality was not on 30 January but a few weeks later, and even then he was provoked into it by the action of someone else. This was the fire at the Reichstag on the evening of 27 February, one of history's great mysteries or so it used to be regarded.

The Reichstag fire is a story rich in drama or maybe in black comedy. At first sight there is no great mystery about it. Soon after nine o'clock in the evening of 27 February, the Debating Chamber in the Reichstag was set on fire. The wooden panelling and the dusty curtains burnt briskly. Within a quarter of an hour the Chamber was gutted. A young Dutch student called Marinus van der Lubbe was found wandering around the building. He at once confessed that he had got in through a broken window just before nine o'clock and had started the fire with the aid of firelighters. When the supply of these gave out he had torn his shirt into strips and set these alight. All this seemed straightforward enough. But not for long.

Hitler and other leading Nazis were at a party nearby. On the news of the fire they rushed off to the Reichstag. As Hitler burst in he announced in a frenzy: 'This is a Communist plot, the signal for an uprising. Every Communist official must be shot. The Communist MPs must be hanged.' From that moment the Reichstag fire was changed from a simple event to a profound mystery, a character it has never lost. For if Hitler, the inspired Führer, had said there was a Communist plot, a Communist plot there must have been. The police reported that there was clear evidence against van der Lubbe and against him alone. Their report was swept aside. Hitler had spoken. The police made little headway in identifying Communist criminals. Torgler, Communist leader in the Reichstag, had been in the building but had been seen to leave well before the fire started. The police also brought in three Bulgarian Communists who happened to be in Berlin – Dimitrov, Popov and Tanev. The police did not know that in Dimitrov they had caught the chief Comintern representative in Western Europe.

There was already another version in circulation. On the first news of the fire Willi Münzenberg, an inspired Communist publicist then living in Paris, announced that the Nazis had set fire to the Reichstag themselves. Every anti-Nazi in Europe from Communist to liberal believed the story without question. Soon two rival shows were running. The Nazis laid on a trial before the German Supreme Court in Leipzig. Münzenberg and others organised a counter-trial in London. The rival shows ran for a long time. The Nazis handled their show badly, proof perhaps that the fire had taken them by surprise. They failed to produce the slightest evidence against any of the accused except van der Lubbe, who repeatedly insisted that he had done it all alone. Faced with evidence from so-called experts that this was impossible, he replied: 'I was there and they were not.' For some strange reason they brought in Goering as a witness and this gave Dimitrov the opportunity to harass the witness ruthlessly. The Supreme Court timidly preserved its independence. Though it rejected van der Lubbe's evidence, it found him alone guilty. The four Communists were released.

Meanwhile the counter-trial flourished in London. Münzenberg was a master in manufacturing evidence. He produced alleged Nazi renegades to tell their fabulous stories. He even produced a detailed letter of confession from a Nazi who was killed in Hitler's 'blood-bath' of 30 June 1934. According to these witnesses, the Nazi complicity in the fire turned on a tunnel which led from the Speaker's house to the Reichstag. Goering was now the Speaker. The Nazis were so bemused by this story that they showed the tunnel to journalists in an effort to prove that it was for water pipes, not for human beings. Willi Münzenberg's story is still widely accepted. Most people, if questioned, would say that the Nazis set fire to the Reichstag if they gave any answer at all. They would be wrong. Van der Lubbe set fire to the Reichstag all alone. But it is very unlikely that the truth will prevail. Indeed, there are still ingenious people who offer to reveal the real secret of the Reichstag fire. But they never do so.

12

Here is a story with a warning. For years past, as I drove from King's Cross to the Angel, I have noticed St James's Church, Pentonville, at the top of the hill and have promised myself that one day I would pay it a visit. I was in too much of a hurry or the traffic was too dense or it was beginning to rain – there was always some excuse for pushing by. On the one occasion I actually stopped, the church was locked, which is for ever happening with churches nowadays. I was confident that St James's would always be there. It was a small church and its upkeep could not cost much. It was by way of being a church of some fame: Grimaldi was buried there and the theatrical profession could surely be counted on to maintain it. Above all, it was an adornment to an otherwise undistinguished site.

Now what do I learn? The custodians of the church – whether the local authorities or the Church authorities I am not sure – have so neglected the church that it has become a slum and must be pulled down. The truth is that neither the local authorities nor the Church can be trusted with buildings of any past or character. Local authorities hate any buildings put up before yesterday. Now the Church authorities, once the guardians of tradition, are equally destructive. Look at their treatment of something far more sacred than St James's Church, Pentonville: the Authorised Version of the Bible. This is the most treasured work in all English literature. It is the foundation of our culture. And what has the Established Church done with it? The Authorised Version has been practically obliterated. It is rarely read in church; it is never used in schools, particularly not in Church schools. None of my grandchildren, all now passing through state schools, has ever opened an Authorised Version of the Bible. They are not aware that it exists. Such is the way in which the Established Church has discharged its trust. The culminating irony of the situation is that the New English Bible, having superseded the Authorised Version, has not taken its place. The New Bible is so dreary and flat that no one reads it. Children nowadays are offered fairy stories that have some vague connection with the Bible. Adults do not read the Bible at all. As to St James's Church, Pentonville, the moral of that story is that one should never put off visiting a church of interest. Otherwise it will disappear before you get around to it.

I was recently invited to celebrate one of the most significant days or, to be exact, evenings of my life. Twenty-five years ago, on 17 February 1958, the original Campaign for Nuclear Disarmament held its inaugural meeting in the Central Hall, Westminster. I offered to speak, and my offer was accepted, though rather casually: I was put at the bottom of the list when all the great figures such as Bertrand Russell and Michael Foot had gone home. However, for some reason I put the audience in a frenzy. After I had finished and gone home, the audience swarmed out and laid siege to No 10 Downing Street. It was a very satisfactory start to the Campaign for Nuclear Disarmament.

For the next two years there was rarely a week when I did not speak at one or more mass meetings. I estimate that I have spoken in more public halls than either Gladstone or John Bright did, if only because some of the halls were not built in their day. After about two years I ran out of cities or great towns to visit, and I also ran out of steam as to what to say. I was delighted at the prospect of celebrating the beginning of my career with CND. My delight did not last long. I was a few minutes late at the gathering. Evidently the celebration was already over or perhaps it had never taken place. At all events, no one mentioned the events, now far distant, at the Central Hall. No one remarked to me that I had played some part in the original meeting. Like the meeting, I was forgotten. I observed that CND is now feminist in spirit and composition. After that, I left abruptly, an unsuccessful mission.

Actually, I had some slight conversation. One young man, not even born when the meeting of 1958 had taken place, asked what answer I had to Mrs Thatcher's remark that if Hitler had had an atomic bomb he would have used it. What had CND to say to that? To judge from Hitler's usual behaviour, Hitler would certainly have used the atomic bomb if the Germans had possessed it. He

119

would not have been deterred by the threat of British retaliation, even if the British had also possessed the secret. Hitler used the rockets, which were troublesome enough. He was not deterred by the Allied bombing of Dresden, which was quite as catastrophic as a 1945-style atomic bomb. This merely goes to show that if an antagonist possesses nuclear bombs and determines to use them he will not be deterred by any threat of retaliation. It is usually thought that the Japanese were driven to sue for peace by the atomic bombs dropped on Hiroshima and Nagasaki. In fact, the Japanese had already decided to sue for peace. The bombs were not dropped to end the war – that was already under way. They were dropped on the insistence of nuclear scientists, in order to demonstrate to Congress that the money spent on developing the bombs had not been wasted. There is only one remedy for nuclear weapons: don't have them. The result cannot be worse than the possession of them will be.

I have a celebration to chronicle far more memorable than any CND meeting. February 23 marked the 350th anniversary of the birth of Samuel Pepys. Something more. By a happy chance, the occasion marks also the completion of the publication of Pepys's Diary by Robert Latham. Strictly speaking, publication of the actual Diary was completed with Volume 9 in 1976. What now crowns the work is Volume 10, the Companion, composed of miscellaneous though relevant essays, and Volume 11, the Index.* In my opinion, Pepys's Diary, as now published, is the finest work of English scholarship in our lifetime. It is complete, as no previous edition of the Diary has been: it is a perfect transcription, which is also new, and its editing, especially the notes, adds to its value. I read the volumes as they came out from 1970 to 1976, and am now looking forward to the Companion. I say without hesitation that the Diary is the most attractive work in the English language. If I were ever fool enough to go to a desert island it is undoubtedly the work I should take with me. As it is, I hope to read the Diary all through once again before I die.

Pepys's Diary has a special character. Pepys was a competent civil servant who devoted his life to the service of the Admiralty Board. He wrote his Diary in his spare time. He showed it to no one. Indeed, so far as I can tell, he never reopened it himself. The

* Bell and Hyman.

Diary was a whim, a hobby. He wrote it conscientiously almost every day for nine years. Then he gave it up on a sudden alarm that he was losing his sight. The alarm turned out to be false, but he never returned to his Diary and never wrote any more. He served in the Admiralty for another twenty years. Then, having remained faithful to James II, he was ousted by the Glorious Revolution and spent the rest of his life in contented retirement.

Pepys produces some impressive set-pieces, such as the Restoration of Charles II in 1660 or the great Fire of London in 1666. Most of the Diary chronicles the events of everyday life: social occasions, visits to the theatre, domestic cares and amorous adventures, not very serious. He was often called to order by his somewhat overbearing wife, which he accepted as one of the inevitable events in his life. Pepys gives a first impression of being a very ordinary man, a conscientious public servant doing all the normal things. On further reflection, Pepys stands out as a unique figure. No one has ever produced a Diary like his, and no one ever will. I have lived long enough to have a perfect text of the Diary provided for me. How grateful I am to Robert Latham and William Matthews.

I have happy domestic news to report. My wife is safely back from hospital. Her malady has passed over, even though the doctors are not sure what was the cause of it. I do not like leading a solitary existence in an otherwise empty house. I do not like preparing my solitary dinners or drinking my solitary wine. With my wife's return I have some special enjoyments. For the first week after her return she stayed in bed for breakfast. There is nothing I like more than taking up my wife's breakfast. And none of those Continental breakfasts which are hardly worth preparing. I produce every day a traditional English breakfast. I take up half a grapefruit straight away, properly segmented, to keep my wife busy while I prepare what is to follow. I grind the coffee and drip it through a cafetière. I grill rashers of bacon, accompanied each day by variations of tomato, mushrooms or eggs. Every now and then, I interrupt the routine with half a grilled kipper each – I think my favourite breakfast. I rarely stray to finnan haddock, though I like that too. On Sunday mornings we have the special treat of real porridge as a preliminary, simmered for half an hour or more the night before and then heated up again the following morning. Of course, I get the same joy in making the breakfast when my wife comes down for it, but it gives special enjoyment to rush each course upstairs while it is hot.

Breakfast is my prime achievement of the day. Lunch means biscuits and cheese, which even the most inexperienced amateur can turn out. Tea means only a crumpet with Gentleman's Relish. We eat this every day, though it is rather greedy to do so. Soon the period of crumpets will come to an end: I think immediately before Easter when hot cross buns take its place. As to dinner, I am afraid I run upstairs, get detailed instructions and then run downstairs again. I apply this technique to every course, and ultimately dinner is produced, though not up to my wife's standard. The essential thing is that she is back with me and my life is once more an uninterrupted round of happiness.

13

I recently celebrated my 77th birthday. I don't know why I should describe myself as celebrating it. Celebrations of my birthday seem long ago now. I have a photograph of myself on my 13th, wearing a new Eton jacket and a starched collar. I am looking pleased enough, but appearances are misleading: I vaguely recollect that I did not like the Eton jacket and doubt whether I ever wore it again. My mother intended that I should go to juvenile balls. I never learnt to dance and therefore never accepted invitations. The Eton jacket languished unworn.

I remember a very enjoyable dinner in Oxford on the occasion of my 21st birthday. The guests included Norman Cameron and Tom Driberg, now both dead, and 'Michael Innes', still alive. We had dinner in a private room at the George restaurant, now also dead. Halfway through dinner the waiter asked to speak to me in private. Then he said: 'I am a respectable married man and if that gentleman comes out again I shall go home.' I expostulated with Tom, who restrained his curiosity for the rest of the evening. I reminded Tom of this episode shortly before he died. He remembered the waiter perfectly and said: 'Why did he say he was a respectable married man? I wonder what that had to do with it.'

I remember also a dinner party some years later when I was living in Vienna. We had another private room, this time at Sacher's – much grander than the George and also much cheaper. There were some English friends whom I had got to know in Vienna and also my girlfriend, Else. Soon after this dinner my innocent friendship with Else came to an end. Her family discovered that I was taking her to a restaurant when she made out that we were going to a cinema. Apparently it was wicked for an unmarried girl to dine alone with a man, and Else was forbidden ever to see me again. We resumed our friendship just the other day. Touching.

On my 70th birthday I was given a lunch at the LSE by some of my younger friends. The party was graced by the presence of Michael Foot and Lord Blake. Soon afterwards Robert Blake struck me off his visiting-list because I had opposed the witch-hunt at the British Academy against Anthony Blunt. I am glad to record that Blake has now forgiven me, or perhaps he thinks I have purged my offence. At any rate, I am now restored to favour.

Of course, I am pleased to provide an occasion when other people enjoy themselves – it is a bit hard to expect me to join in the rejoicings:

But at my back I always hear
Time's wingèd chariot hurrying near.

No, that is not quite right. I am not worried at all about the approach of death. It is becoming for me the order of release. I hope I shall have a painless death. But there is nothing to be apprehensive about in death itself. What begins to trouble me is the approach of old age. This has come upon me quite recently. When I was 70 I was as fit as when I was 21. I last went up Coniston Old Man when I was 72. I consoled myself with the recollection of James Tait, that great historian, who last went up Scafell when he was 84. Now my body is beginning to let me down. I used to be able to walk from the local bus terminal to Kenwood House without difficulty at a smart pace. Now it takes me all afternoon to get up Parliament Hill. I walk slowly. I easily become unsteady. I feel dizzy and have to sit down. In a bus or Underground a youngster occasionally gives me a seat – very rarely, I must say. I am inclined to fall asleep in the afternoon. Alternatively, I wake up at four or five in the morning and cannot go to sleep again.

I have many consolations. I drive a car as efficiently as I did sixty years ago, which is when I started to drive. But I don't enjoy it much. My sight is undimmed, except that I have to use different glasses for reading. My appetite is excellent and so is my digestion. I drink half a bottle of wine every day and plenty of beer as well. And that reminds me of a serious problem. For many years I bought each year a few cases of claret which I deposited with

124

Avery's in Bristol. Now I have started to drink this stock. But how fast should I go? I should look a damned fool if I ran through my reserve before I died. But I should look even more foolish if I died with some of my reserve untapped. There is no easy answer.

I cannot complain that much of old age as yet. For most of the day I do not notice old age at all. But then it comes upon me: pains in the back, hesitation on the feet. It is all sure to get worse. How well Arthur Koestler arranged things: just my age and then passed peacefully away. I too should like to indent for a death pill. If all other claims fail I could justify an issue of death pills as a precaution against nuclear warfare, which is rapidly approaching. I am afraid it is hopeless. I look at my wife across the dinner table. She needs me. She loves me. For her sake I suppose I must endure life as long as I can. Still, it is a great nuisance.

People used to wish me many happy returns, which is acceptable enough, though it is becoming rather pointless. But now total strangers accompany their good wishes with appeals to my charity: requests for a contribution to some more or less worthy purpose, quite often straightforward requests for money and, most tiresome of all, requests for copies of my books. It does not occur to these people that I have no more spare copies of my books than they have. None of them gets a book, or, for that matter, any money. They ought to be sending money to me.

I must confess that I have recently had much to make my life enjoyable. Pre-eminent was *Heartbreak House*, which I saw at the Haymarket. I have little doubt that it is Shaw's best play, certainly better than that overrated work *Man and Superman*. Who cares whether Ann Whitefield marries Jack Tanner or not? *Heartbreak House* has real people behaving as real people should. Critics have expressed some dissatisfaction with Rex Harrison as Captain Shotover. I thought he was perfect. A further merit about *Heartbreak House* is that it has no message. All Shaw's plays are full of talk, but usually it has relevance to something. In *Heartbreak House* they just talk. The flaw in the play is the episode of the Zeppelin raid, which Shaw stuck in at the end to show he had written the play during the war – which he hadn't. It is clear that he had no idea what a real air-raid was like. The play confirmed my opinion that Shaw is our greatest playwright since Shakespeare. No, perhaps that is wrong. Shakespeare is irrelevant to Shaw. He

125

was our greatest playwright since Ben Jonson. People will be listening to Shaw's plays when we are living for two or is it three hundred years – *vide Back to Methuselah*. What a dreadful prospect, by the way.

I cannot let the centenary of Karl Marx's death pass without notice. He is by no means forgotten. *The Communist Manifesto* sells more copies than it did in his lifetime, particularly in the United States. I know. I wrote an introduction to the Penguin edition of the *Manifesto* in 1967 and this has brought me a handsome payment of royalties ever since. The *Manifesto* deserves its success, or rather the first two chapters do. The concluding two are a hasty botch, never finished because Marx left to take part in the German revolution of 1848. Marx never returned to the *Manifesto*: he did not even bother to correct the proofs of the German edition, which still circulates as it came out in 1848. In fact, Marx attached no importance to his most famous work.

What else is left of his reputation? No doubt it is still well-known that he wrote a ponderous book on the workings of the capitalist system. But how many people read it? Some may struggle through the first volume, which Marx more or less completed. It contains some lively passages on the horrors of capitalism, but the demonstration of how the worker is robbed at the point of production no longer carries conviction. Volumes Two and Three were left in a chaos on Marx's death. Apparently Marx had been busy collecting material for a study of Balzac and did no work on *Capital* in his declining years. Engels tried to make some sense of the confusion. He was not very successful. I read all three volumes some sixty years ago: very wisely, I have never returned to them and do not propose to do so now. I wonder if the directors of Soviet economic policy use the three volumes of *Capital* as their daily handbook. I rather think not.

Marx's historical writings still make good reading, which is more than can be said of his economic writing. This is particularly true of *The Eighteenth Brumaire of Louis Napoelon* and *The Civil War in France*, about the Paris Commune of 1871, both of them brilliant historical pamphlets. This does not necessarily imply that the history in them is reliable. There is also merit in Marx's journalistic writing on foreign affairs, especially on the Crimean War when Marx was passionately on the side of Turkey against Russia. He even accused Palmerston, the British Foreign Secretary, of being a Russian agent. This was not the last time that such accusations were made.

As to Marx's philosophical writings, I find them unreadable. I wonder whether even Comrade Andropov has read *The Poverty of Philosophy*, to say nothing of *The German Ideology*. Perhaps no other man has owed his reputation to books which nobody reads or has ever heard of. It is also curious that before Marx died he had ceased to be a Communist and was a warm patron of the German Social Democratic Party.

14

I have recently read *The History Men* by John Kenyon. I remember reading a different book, *The History Man* by Malcolm Bradbury, some years ago. I did not find Bradbury's book at all funny, which I am told it is intended to be. After a careful reading I had not the slightest inkling of what the book was supposed to be about. Indeed I thought my mind was going. There is no such problem about Kenyon's book. It is a well-written, straightforward account of how English history has been written in England during the last three or four hundred years. John Kenyon is very competent, very fair. He does not seem to have any favourite, though he admits that Gibbon, not a writer of English history, has slipped in because he was the greatest of English historians. Quite right, I think, even though Gibbon hardly passes any of the present-day tests. He never looked at a single manuscript text. He did not know that the past is different from the present. He captures the reader with his wit rather than his scholarship, though that is pretty good as well.

Otherwise Kenyon writes only on those who wrote about English history. The result is one of the funniest books I have ever read. The individual historians whom Kenyon presents have usually been conscientious scholars devoted to the muse of history. Some of them were even accurate about their facts. But the Profession, as Kenyon calls it, is incurably comic. I can think of nothing else in the intellectual field that has provoked so much controversy and venom over the centuries. Maybe the biologists were as virulent at the height of the Darwin controversy. But their row did not last very long. The historians have been at it for centuries and are still disputing as lavishly as ever. The topics of dispute have varied; the energy flung into them has remained the same.

Though the writing of history has gone on for a long time, the profession of history is quite recent. Gibbon was not a professional historian – he was a gentleman of leisure who wrote history for fun. Macaulay, on the other hand, wrote history for money and earned sums unparalleled until the present day. The 19th century was the best time for historians. In those days an historian was a man who wrote works of history and the works were of inordinate length. No nonsense about the historian teaching young students – that was done by hacks who were not qualified to do anything else. Nowadays the historian is so busy tutoring, lecturing and sitting on committees that he has virtually no time to write books at all. Then think of the great names that adorn the 19th century: Carlyle, Freeman, Froude, Seely, Acton. They usually disliked each other. Froude was an exception in that he idolised Carlyle: but this did not prevent his writing a highly libellous biography of Carlyle after the latter's death. Acton also was an exception in that unlike the others he did not write anything at all. I am glad to say this has now consigned him to oblivion – one of the great frauds of Christendom.

Historians nowadays have to spend much of their time in trivial tasks but I am glad to report that it is possible to write substantial works of history if you skimp your other work. I know: I have written thirty works of history over a period of just under fifty years. I am also glad to report that contemporary historians are as controversial as their 19th-century predecessors. What they dispute over are new methods of history which have nothing to do with narrative. I am at a loss over this. I think that history has no purpose unless it answers the child's question, 'What happened next?' This rules me out of serious consideration. Not that I mind. I write history for fun and have done all my life.

I have just seen a great film. I saw it in unpropitious circumstances – a community centre with a sheet as screen. I thought *Closely Observed Trains* the best film I had ever seen when I first saw it years ago. I thought the same when I saw it a few days ago. It is incomparable in its simplicity. The original story is by a Czech writer, Bohumil Hrabal. It should certainly be translated into English. It does not diminish its grandeur that there was very little sabotage by the Czechs during the Second World War.

It is very rare for me to see a film and even rarer to see two quite close together. My excuse is that I saw the second on television and not a good print at that. The film was *Sunset Boulevard*, the film put on in honour of Gloria Swanson when she died. It was a very daring gesture for an aging film star to inspire a film about a decaying film star. It was an even more daring gesture to parade the melodrama of her younger years. I don't think Gloria Swanson could have carried it alone. What nearly made *Sunset Boulevard* a great film was Erich von Stroheim, one of whose finest performances this was. Perhaps male actors do not age as rapidly as women or maybe they can become different but still brilliant personalities. At any rate there he was in full glory. The climax comes when von Stroheim calls 'Action!' to the waiting press photographers and he called it as vividly as he did sixty years before. My memories of von Stroheim go back to *Blind Husbands* and *Foolish Wives*. One of the two, I forget which, ends with von Stroheim being dropped down a manhole. I cannot remember any film by Gloria Swanson but I once met her on a television chat show and she was delightful company – sensible and unassuming. I said to her afterwards: 'Miss Swanson, I have been waiting for fifty years to express my admiration of you.' It was not true but it gave her pleasure and she deserved it.

I do not like Abroad. It took me a long time to realise this. Year after year I went on sight-seeing trips or 'did' some foreign city. In this earnest way I have 'done' Rome, Paris, Florence, Amsterdam and countless more. Now I have written off these pursuits of culture. I go to Budapest because my wife's sons live there. Some time soon I shall visit Vienna to renew acquaintance with old friends and with one particular friend once dear to me. But no more tramps round cities with a Companion guide.

There is one exception to this sweeping renunciation of foreign tours. Every time I visit Venice I like it more. The absence of motor-cars transforms it into an Elysium, something quite unimaginable until you get there. It is of course also an asset that there are some things to see. I am not keen on the paintings, though everyone tells me that they are very good. I have never managed to see a Tintoretto. I have looked at Tintoretto's famous pictures but they are all so dark that I can never see them. I give the prize to Carpaccio and he takes only a couple of hours. Otherwise I keep clear of the Accademia and still more of the famous churches. As to St Mark's it is quite incomprehensible. There are two churches which rank among the finest in the world: S. Maria dei Miracoli and, even finer, S. Nicolo dei Mendicoli, which has recently recaptured its ancient splendour.

I have just spent a delightful week in Venice and yet I must confess it is within sight of ruin. Instead of motor-cars it is being ruined by an excess of people, particularly parties of schoolchildren. The little brutes are everywhere, screaming and shouting. They display not the slightest interest in the buildings they are supposed to be visiting: they just rush on all the more wildly. Their teacher or whoever is in charge of them makes no attempt to explain what they are looking at or to stir up their interest. It is enough that they can be kept on the noisy move. Schoolchildren should be taken to see things that interest them, such as football matches. Venice should be preserved from the under-twenties.

I suppose I ought to make some comment on Hitler's alleged diaries. Unlike my historical colleagues, I do not hurry into print with some easy answer. It would take me months if not years of work to arrive at the truth. Maybe I never would. The question is of little importance. The diaries, even if authentic, make little modification in the historical record . . . Indeed they make none at all. Who cares about Hitler nowadays? He has become a sort of prehistoric monster. I am inclined to dismiss the diaries as an ingenious forgery. Now if these were Stalin's diaries . . .

15

As I write this paragraph the General Election is still almost four weeks away, and yet it seems already to have stolen the show. There is nothing else to read in the newspapers of any significance. My problem is that the General Election itself is of singularly little significance. No one in his senses imagines that the result will make the slightest difference. We have lived in the shadow of two great problems for the last ten years and more. One is unemployment; the other is inflation. To my mind, inflation is the more catastrophic of the two because it saps the very foundations of civilisation. Maybe I think this because I am too old and too lucky to be affected by unemployment. At any rate, there are the two great problems and neither of our two parties has the slightest idea what to do about them. Does anyone suppose that if the Conservatives win the election they will do any better than they have done for the last few years? Does anyone suppose that if Labour wins the election they will improve on their previous record when in office? They tell me that there is some sort of jumped-up third party, but I don't think we need bother about that. Third parties rarely succeed. I can only think of the Labour Party between the wars and it has run out of steam now.

In short, the General Election is likely to be more barren than any of its predecessors during my lifetime. Looking back, I can recollect one which we thought really would make a difference. That was the General Election of 1945. I did a good deal of speaking during that election. I won't say that we thought that the revolution was just round the corner, but something pretty near it. The high expectation survived for two or three years and then ran away to nothing. After that we have never had confident morning again.

The present General Election seems peculiarly pointless. The

Government has nothing to offer except a continuation of its record of failure. The Labour alternative carries little conviction. The only justification for voting at all is that the rival parties are no worse than they have been for almost forty years past. Or perhaps they are. The winning ticket is likely to give permission to do worse than anything that has gone before and we shall settle down in resignation. There is one problem for which I believe there is a solution, and yet no one does anything about it. That is Ireland. People are killed there every week. Indeed the death rate goes up. There have been feeble initiatives and they have all died away. There is, I believe, a simple solution and that is Troops Out. The killing started when the British troops were sent to Ulster years ago. It is just possible that it will stop when the British troops go away. At any rate, British troops will no longer be killed when they are no longer there.

I do not need to add that there is also a solution for the problem of nuclear weapons, and that is not to have them. This problem has been going the rounds for twenty years past and the solution has been on offer also. It is a strange idea that our country, or for that matter any other country, will be the stronger for having the capacity to murder the helpless civilian population of other countries. Those who prepare and plan nuclear war have nothing to be afraid of. They will be comfortably settled in nuclear shelters and will be safe from all harm. There will be one consolation for those of us who are already dead. The warmongers who have survived the nuclear war will emerge to find an uninhabitable world, and quite soon they will perish even more miserably than we have done. Clearly this is not a topic to be debated at a general election.

I turn to a more agreeable subject. I have just published a book. During the last ten years I have published volumes of essays and illustrated books. But my last real book was my life of Beaverbrook, which I published more than ten years ago. Now I have done something even more personal. I have published a book about myself. To my delight, I discovered that I had a good memory, and what is more, a memory of a visual kind. My past unrolled before me like a series of lantern slides. I can recall, say, the face of Kinder Scout or the buildings of Rievaulx Abbey. I am not so good with the appearance of human beings – perhaps they are constantly changing. But I can remember the back streets of

Manchester or the Ghetto in Venice. These memories fill my mind when I am no longer able to re-stock them in real life. I can recall also conversations that took place twenty or forty years ago. At least I can recall the sight of people talking – I am less sure of what they are saying. I suspect that most of the conversations have an element of invention or perhaps 'adornment' is the better word.

How does my life look in the perspective of more than seventy years? There have been periods of boredom and occasional periods of distress, but mainly I can report that I have had lots of fun. I have not achieved anything of great substance: thirty or so books of history, some of them, I think, quite good, but all of them destined to be forgotten within a relatively few years; and a long run as a public entertainer. I cannot put my television appearances under any other heading. The achievements I am most proud of apart from my books are two lectures: the Ford Lectures given as long ago as 1957, and the Romanes Lecture given in 1982 – both, I need hardly say, without a script or notes. I have never achieved academic eminence except that honorary degrees are now showered upon me. It gives me more pleasure that taxi-drivers call me 'Alan'.

What shall I be able to quote at the imaginary Day of Judgment? I drove a car for Preston Strike Committee during the General Strike of 1926. I spoke against the Hoare-Laval plan in 1935 and against the Munich conference in 1938. I also applauded the mass trespass on Kinder Scout in, I think, 1933, though I did not take part in it. After the Second World War I opposed the Cold War and have gone on doing so ever since. I formulated the Yugoslav claim to Trieste, though without success. I opposed the Korean War almost from the first day. And opposed the Suez aggression of 1956 even more passionately. Indeed I imagined I and my like would be committed to war resistance. It all turned out a false alarm. From 1958 to 1961 I served almost full time in the Campaign for Nuclear Disarmament. This is the only thing that will get me acquitted at the Day of Judgment.

In a different sphere, I am proud to have walked the Pennine Way and Offa's Dyke Way, neither of them quite completely. I'd throw in the Fairfield Horse Shoe as the best day's walk I have ever made. They are all beyond me now: my greatest pleasure is to sit in the sun when there is any, and what could be more agreeable than

134

that? Oh, I have forgotten, there is something better – eating and drinking. As long as these hold out, I shall want to go on living. But I am on the home run.

For some weeks now and for some more to come I have been engaged in a formidable task. I have been reading Volume VI of Martin Gilbert's Life of Winston Churchill. An alarming notice on the cover warns me of the most terrifying penalties if I divulge anything the volume contains. But I think I can risk stating that the volume starts in September 1939 and runs until December 1941. There is also another starting date: 10 May 1940, when Churchill became Prime Minister and virtually the dictator of the country. This became clearer to me the more I read. There have been strong prime ministers before and maybe since. But there has been none who actually ran the whole show. Churchill had colleagues. He had assistants and advisers, many of them of great ability. But in the last resort everything depended on him. He was the mainspring without which the machinery of state would not work.

The more one reads, the more extraordinary his achievement becomes. The intensity of Churchill's interest no doubt varied from subject to subject, but he was capable of picking up some new subject that he had apparently forgotten and knew nothing about. Of course he made mistakes. He invented plans civil and military that did not come off. He missed some chances, though not many. But it is hardly an exaggeration to say that for fifteen months or so Churchill directed the entire Second World War on the so-called Allied side. Napoleon did something similar for France in the early 19th century, but not on the same scale. Churchill's field of action was more limited once Stalin and Roosevelt were added to the War Lords: it was still true that Churchill ran the entire British war, at any rate, to the very end.

He acknowledged only two authorities: the King and Parliament, meaning the House of Commons. But the War Cabinet was primarily a gathering of colleagues who followed Churchill's guidance. The physical achievement alone was staggering. No doubt it exhausted him, but he lasted another ten years. Churchill's accomplishment was without parallel in modern times and no man could have exercised a dictatorship with more moderation.

Reading this volume puts another thought into my mind. The Second World War was the noblest task to which the British people ever set their hand. We alone on the Allied side entered the war of our voluntary choice and stayed in it till the end. No war has been fought for such noble motives. Yet it was hardly over before it was set aside and soon forgotten. When I finished my *Second World War: An Illustrated History* with the words, 'Despite all the killing and destruction that accompanied it, the Second World War was a good war,' a junior colleague rebuked me sternly and I felt quite ashamed. On reflection I still think it was a good war.

16

Quite a time has passed since I last contributed a Diary to the *London Review of Books*, so long indeed that I have almost forgotten how to do it. Was my mind once flooding over with possible themes? I can hardly believe it. Certainly my mind is empty now. I stir my memory in vain. Here are some oddities that occur to me. The oddest is the persistence with which readers of the *London Review of Books* accuse me of supporting the wrong side in the Cold War and in particular of taking a sympathetic view of Hungary and its problems. The accusation about the Cold War is merely silly. I am against the Cold War and all that goes with it, as much against the Russians waging the Cold War, if they do, as against the Americans. The Cold War is a competition in obstinate misunderstanding. I doubt whether either side can remember how the Cold War started or what it is now about. They just go on parading their mutual distrust until it has become a way of life, and neither side will be satisfied until it has provoked a world explosion. I humbly think this is a mistake, but there is no limit to the extent of human folly.

As to Hungary, it had an obscurantist regime in the days of Regent Horthy and it was a great stroke for Hungary when the Horthy regime was overthrown. There followed a bad period under Rakosi, a period which ended in the upheaval of 1956. There was a revolution that was carried too far and then a rebound. Nowadays Hungary, despite economic difficulties, has a settled way of life and a civilised culture. I am married to a Hungarian, I go to Hungary quite often. My impression is that Hungarian society is nearer to the bourgeois English culture of the early 20th century than it is to either of the two monsters, Russian or American. When I first went to Hungary I looked everywhere for the horrors of Communism. I am looking still and not finding any anywhere.

Certainly I am not likely to change my views because of abusive letters in the *London Review of Books*.

I have recently published a book, my autobiography, called *A Personal History*. The reviews have been for the most part highly flattering and I found the critical reviews for the most part more flattering than the others. One reviewer claimed that the book was 'egocentric'. What else could it be? I had assumed rightly or wrongly that an autobiography ought to be about myself, hence egocentric, and as a matter of fact I incline to think that my book is not egocentric enough. Of course I can tell stories about what happened to me, but I have never found anything interesting to report about the state and development of my mind. One phrase surprised and indeed shocked me. I was described as the Macaulay of the 20th century. Whoever coined that phrase had never read Macaulay. I am not worthy to kiss the hem of Macaulay's garment. If a comparison is wanted I should describe myself as the Marriott of the 20th century. Sir John Marriott wrote textbooks of 19th and 20th-century history. They are fairly competent and duller than mine but they enabled me to pass examinations. Marriott was also Conservative MP for York, hence a more successful politician. He was slightly to the right of Sir Charles Oman, the other historian MP of the early 20th century. They are now both forgotten, as no doubt I shall be in a few years. I think my books are better than Marriott's but that is probably because they are more left-wing – or are they? A comment on my book of a different kind came recently from a bus conductor. A friend of mine was travelling on a 24 bus carrying *A Personal History* when the conductor tapped him on the shoulder and said: 'He's a good man and he travels sometimes on my bus.' That is a higher compliment than I have received from any reviewer. Now the tumult of reviews is over and I must somehow discover the excessive number of misprints that I have allowed to slip through.

Last time I wrote this Diary the General Election was merely in the offing. Now it has come and gone. So far as I can tell it has not made the slightest difference. The Social Democratic Party has had a severe setback, which is all to the good. I trust this hotchpotch of a party will expire before the next general election. Incidentally, how much David Owen must be regretting that the SDP is still alive. If he had remained in the Labour Party nothing could have prevented his becoming its leader. Perhaps the Executive Committee of the Labour Party could dispatch a telegram saying: 'Come back, David. All is forgiven.' As it is, we are faced with a competition between four or so candidates, none of whom is qualified to be the leader of the Labour Party. Of course the Labour Party is not good at producing a leader. I calculate that there have been only two good leaders of the Party since it made its real start at the end of the First World War. Ramsay MacDonald was the first and he ended by making a lamentable false move. Clem Attlee was the second and he was too careful about his moves ever to make a false one.

As to the Conservative Party, it stands for nothing beyond a desire to discipline the Trade Unions, which will only make the Trade Unions more out of hand than ever. The Government can choose between reducing inflation and reducing unemployment. The more it succeeds with one the more it increases the other, a dilemma from which there is no escape. Of course, Mrs Thatcher can press the button, a course of action she is for ever promising. This would murder some few million Europeans and would provoke an even greater murder of English people. But at least it would end the dreary show.

I turn with relief to more cheerful subjects. I have just spent my annual fortnight at Yarmouth, Isle of Wight. The little town is much as it was in the 18th century, perhaps more so. The few streets are for ever busy and yet there are not too many people about. The holiday camps in the vicinity are remote enough for their users hardly to impinge on Yarmouth at all. There is a Royal Solent Yachting Club, which holds itself highly aloof. There is also a Sailing Club, which is more active. There are always racing dinghies in the Solent and grander yachts departing on cross-Channel journeys. There are car ferries arriving every hour as though from foreign parts. I have been going to Yarmouth for thirty years and have never missed a year. In early times I went in winter as well as summer. Now it is too much trouble. I stay in a corn mill built in the 18th century and now adapted to live in. There are allegedly 25 bedrooms on the upper floors, though I have never penetrated so far. My offspring bring their children down as soon as the school holidays begin, just as I used to do. Now the arrival of my grandchildren is the signal for my departure – much as I love

139

them. There are very good walks on the Downs, usually solitary. There is a good local beach on the Solent, slightly pebbly. There is an extensive sandy beach on the other side of the island. In June the beaches are empty, though the sea is already warm. Altogether, Yarmouth is an ideal place to retire to. I am glad I have spent so much of my life in it.

I have at last discovered a topic of public policy. This is the House of Lords – if that can be regarded as still a matter of public concern. I thought it had ceased to exist long ago. Not at all. Mrs Thatcher wants to create eight or nine more peers. Michael Foot, as a final gesture of leadership, wants to create 29. What can be the explanation of this extraordinary demand? Once upon a time the Leader of the Labour movement was solid against the House of Lords. Can you imagine Keir Hardie as a peer? Surprising and highly creditable, when MacDonald resigned as prime minister, King George proposed to admit him to the Order of the Thistle. MacDonald refused on the ground that he would have to be called 'Sir'. Now, elderly Labour figures fight to be called 'My Lord'. What justification is there nowadays for a House of Lords? There is perhaps some case for a revising chamber, but it should be composed of legal experts, not of Lords and Ladies. The present House of Lords is not competent to revise except by accident. Its function is to preserve the aristocratic traditions of the old House. The life peers exist to give a spurious air of modern enlightenment. Often the life peers are more aristocratic in their bearing than the hereditary peers, and most of them are so old that they should have been discharged from active service long ago. Others consist of ambitious politicians who dislike the trouble of getting themselves elected. It is lamentable that a politician as enlightened as Michael Foot should have mixed in the House of Lords in any way. Not that the House of Commons is much improvement.

Here is a little practical problem. We have been invaded. A large ginger cat has taken virtual possession of our backyard, which we somewhat fancifully call a patio. Originally it sat on the top of the wall, staring at the birds in the nearby tree and occasionally attempting to catch one of them. In this it did not succeed. Now it has abandoned the hunt and spends the entire day alseep on our little patch of grass. I have always loved cats. During the now remote world war I had a white Siamese cat who was my best friend for many years. This invader is not friendly at all. Any attempt to stroke it or to tickle it under the chin provokes a savage hiss and then a sharp scratch. I do not like this cat at all. But what am I to do? I have no idea where it comes from. Unless violently impelled by a walking-stick, it threatens to remain here permanently. It gets no food from us and apparently none from anyone else. I am fearful that it may die on me. I should look foolish indeed with a dead cat on my hands and no idea who it belongs to. I have courteously conveyed the suggestion that it should go away. No luck so far.

17

I spent almost forty years of my life in Oxford. Seven years ago on my retirement I left Oxford and have hardly ever been there since. Much has changed. Dinner at Magdalen College now has only three courses, an economy which we resisted even during the Second World War. And of course there are girls everywhere. Last time I dined in Magdalen I sat next to a young lady who presented herself to me as a Fellow of the College. I said to her: 'I hope you realise that it is thanks to me you are here. It was I who proposed the emancipating amendment to the College Statutes in 1976.' She was most surprised and said: 'Do you mean to say that once there were no women members of the College? I thought there had been women in Magdalen since its foundation.' So temporary is fame.

I have been thinking what further measure of sexual equality should be introduced in Oxford and have hit on a very desirable one. Parsons' Pleasure, the university bathing-place on the River Cherwell, has existed since way back in the 19th century and it has always been nude, having started before bathing-costumes were invented. There used to be elaborate arrangements to ensure that punts bearing females should not go through Parsons' Pleasure. Instead, the empty punts were piloted through by park attendants. Now these arrangements have lapsed as too expensive, and punts laden with females go through Parsons' Pleasure without a stir. When this first happened the nude male bathers, most of them elderly, plunged into the river every time any girls passed. Now they take no notice. So why not complete the process and turn Parsons' Pleasure into a nude bathing-place for both sexes? Once women are admitted the clientele will soon imagine that they have been there since the beginning of time.

Parsons' Pleasure does not stand alone. It is high time that the sexual inequality at Highgate Ponds was removed. The Ponds have a special swimming-place for men. There is also a substantial enclosure where men can sun-bathe nude. Just outside the enclosure there is a large meadow where bathers can sun-bathe suitably clad. More remotely, there is a very small pond for women, with restricted provision for sun-bathing nude. Its users have to remain flat on their backs. Any nude woman sitting up, or still worse standing, is at once brusquely ordered to lie down – a preposterous arrangement. The women should invade the male enclosure, remove their clothes and sun-bathe there.

I do not despair. Things are on the move even in what were the most conventional places. Torbay, not hitherto known for enlightenment, has decided that it has no objection to girls going topless. Even the police of Torbay can see no legal objection to it. Speed the day when topless girls become acceptable throughout the country. I add a piece of moral guidance I was given in my young days. Some sixty years ago, when I was a schoolboy at York, I attended University Extension Lectures on 'The Greek Way of Life' given by Stoughton Holborn, a figure now forgotten. The most powerful lecture climax I heard from him was: 'To confuse nudity with indecency is the distinguishing mark of the barbarian.' I wonder whether the Greeks really said this. Stoughton Holborn certainly said it with a strong Scotch accent.

Nothing of the slightest interest seems to be happening in public affairs. It would be better to close the whole show down for a year or two. Failing the great world, I can only write about myself. My recent fate has been curious though tiresome. I have fallen a victim to Parkinson's disease. So far as I can understand the disease, it has no known cause. One person contracts it and his neighbour does not. There is no way in which you can take precautions against it and what is more there is no known remedy. There is a drug which probably lessens the impact, but the disease will gradually proceed on its way just the same. The principal symptom is shakiness, at first slight and then more and more troublesome. Often it affects one side more than the other. Being congenitally left-handed, I can hold a teacup or a beer mug with my left hand and it does not shake at all, whereas I have had to give up the use of my right hand almost entirely. One cheerful bit of news is that the disease does not affect my use of a typewriter. Even stranger, it does not affect my driving of a car. On the contrary, when I get out of my car after having driven for some time, I am much steadier than when I got in. But most of the time I am shaking more or less. The most difficult problem is to go downstairs – upstairs not so bad. It is worst when there is no banister or handrail to help me down. Then I have to creep down with my back to the wall, a humiliating process. In a more general way, the disease slows me down physically, though not, of course, mentally. I start out for a walk in quite a spritely fashion and suddenly notice that I can proceed no further. Curiously enough, the effects are usually at their worst when I get up in the morning, and gradually wear off during the day. Another problem, perhaps a result of old age rather than of Parkinson's disease, is that I now wake up around five o'clock in the morning and do not fall asleep again. This is exasperating when I have always prided myself on my capacity to sleep right through the night. Now I toss and turn from dawn onwards. My doctor suggested that I should try a nip of brandy. This makes things worse if anything. Perhaps I do not drink enough.

The workings of the disease are quite unpredictable. I cannot be sure whether I can lecture for a whole hour, indeed whether I can lecture at all. In the course of an evening party I suddenly feel that I can go on no longer and must shakily make my departure. Sometimes I stagger up to bed in the middle of the morning. At other times I go into London and spend most of the day happily reading in the London Library. Gradually I get more reluctant to go out for more than a few hundred yards. I can see that soon I shall be quite content to sit in the open air of my backyard or patio. I lose interest in what is happening further afield.

The latest impact of the disease has thrown out all my plans for the early summer. I had promised to give three lectures to a summer school on Great Britain and Europe in the 20th century. Abruptly it was borne home on me that I could not get to the lecture hall, let alone stand upright for an hour at a time. So all has been cancelled. But I should be sorry to let my thoughts go to waste. Here are some of them.

It is usually held that the 20th century was marked by an increasing estrangement between Great Britain and Germany. The rivalry was attributed to Imperialism, a competition for African colonies. There followed the German building of a great navy which was a threat to Great Britain's maritime supremacy. There were repeated diplomatic crises between the two countries which finally led to war. I have been teaching this for a lifetime. Now I am beginning to think it is a load of old nonsense. There were a few people in Germany preaching hostility towards England, and a few people in England, principally on *The Times*, preaching hostility towards Germany. There were far more pro-Germans in England than there were anti-Germans, and the same applied in Germany the other way round. German bankers in Frankfurt often had a house in Park Lane. The short-lived naval race between England and Germany gradually lost its force as Germany could not keep up. The last disputes, not worth a war in any case, had all been settled by 1914: the British and Germans had agreed to share the Portuguese colonies if these came on the market. The British had also agreed to help finance the Baghdad railway. War between England and Germany never seemed less likely than in July 1914. This sounds wrong-headed. But it is true.

The outbreak of war in August 1914 was not the product of international tensions that had been growing for a long time. War came by mistake. In previous crises over the last forty years, one side or the other had backed down. On this occasion all the powers turned obstinate and could not find a way out. All the same, everyone assumed it would be a quick war. Instead, the war jammed at a deadlock and went on for years. One of the quaintest features of World War One, as it came to be called, is that the respective belligerents were at a loss to define what they were fighting for: 'war aims', as they were called. The French had some cause to hope for Alsace and Lorraine. But was there any sense in the idea that the British should carry on a war for four years in order to acquire the German colonies in Africa? Apart from this, the British found their war aim in the loot of the Ottoman Empire. Surely this could have been done without a four-year war against Germany.

18

My dear friend Gerald, Lord Berners, died in 1950. I thought that not more than half a dozen people remembered him. But the centenary of his birth has brought him back into attention. There have been concerts of his music, performances of his ballets and an exhibition devoted to his life on the fifth floor of the Festival Hall. His two best books have been reprinted in paperback: *First Childhood*, the first part of his autobiography, and *Far from the Madding War*, the best novel written about the Second World War, at any rate in Oxford. This last contains that inspired feature, Emmeline's war work. Emmeline, niece of the head of an Oxford college, had been told that war meant destruction. She bought a priceless 15th-century tapestry, set it up on a frame and unpicked a piece of it every day – the only rational piece of war work ever undertaken.

Gerald had a minor but very good talent, best as a composer but a good writer as well. He also painted on a high level and perhaps best of all he understood the art of living. He had a beautiful house at Faringdon, which he kept modestly open throughout the war. During the week he, too, did war work like Emmeline: he catalogued donations of blood in the basement of the Bodleian Library. At the weekends he had modest parties and superlative food at Faringdon. The coloured pigeons were no longer there, but one could look across the valley to a church tower protruding through the trees. The tower was the last folly in England, built by Berners to improve the view. There was no church and the entrance door was bricked up to avoid the payment of rates imposed by an indignant local council. A retired admiral also wrote to protest, saying that he had been surveying the neighbourhood through his telescope for the last thirty years and that the tower interfered with his view. Gerald wrote back: 'My dear Admiral, If you have been

146

surveying the neighbourhood for thirty years, you must have seen many things that you ought not to have seen.'

Mention of Gerald recalls to my mind that he regularly visited Brixton Prison when Sir Oswald Mosley was interned there as a dangerous Fascist and pro-Hitlerite. When an officious friend warned Gerald that visiting Brixton would bring him, too, under suspicion, Gerald replied, 'It is when a friend is under suspicion that he needs friends most,' and went on visiting Brixton. The treatment of the Mosleys was indeed a scandal. Mosley and Diana made no secret of the fact that they thought British participation in the war against Germany a mistake. This is a view they were entitled to hold. The Government was justified in interning them in the short period when there was a danger, somewhat imaginary, of a German invasion. Even then there was no justification to treat them as common criminals. They were confined in separate prisons – Brixton and Holloway. Each of them was locked up in a dark cell from 4 p.m. to 9 a.m., and this continued long after all danger of invasion had passed. Diana Mosley was feeding a four-month-old child. She refused to take the baby to prison and on the way there stopped at a chemist's to buy a breast pump to get rid of her milk, which was ample. In the panic period everything could perhaps be excused, the treatment of the Mosleys as much as that of the Germans, Jews and Socialists, interned in the Isle of Man.

When the panic passed the internees were gradually released. The Mosleys, though now united at Holloway, were kept in prison until 1943. Gerald used to lunch with them each week. He learnt the recipe of an omelette from Diana and served it regularly at Faringdon House as Omelette Holloway. Gerald could get fun out of everything, a good man and a good friend. I shall miss him and treasure his memory. I and Isaiah Berlin were the only members of Oxford University who attended his cremation.

All this seems long ago. I am, however, delighted to read that the Mosley affair is causing embarrassment to the Government. After Mosley was arrested he was interrogated at length by Sir Norman Birkett, a high-grade barrister who specialised in political inquiries. Birkett was by way of being a left-winger. At any rate, he has a Lake District Fell named after him to commemorate his defence of public access to parts of the Lake District. Clearly he was the man to interrogate Sir Oswald Mosley. But something seems to have gone wrong: and the Home Office is to lock up the records for an indefinite period. Mosley was no mean antagonist. According to the account with which he entertained his friends, the charge that Birkett pressed against Mosley was that he was opposed to the war against Germany. What was wrong with that? Mosley asked. And Mosley then recited the names of those in high places who were opposed to the war. Little did Mosley know how justified his case was.

For instance, on 28 May 1940 the War Cabinet discussed the question whether the British should appeal to Mussolini as an intermediary with Hitler. Lord Halifax, the Foreign Secretary, was keen on this or as keen as he could be on anything. Neville Chamberlain, until recently Prime Minister, supported Halifax. Arthur Greenwood, a recent Labour addition, dismissed the idea, as Clement Attlee did more cautiously. Churchill, the Prime Minister, said the idea would not work. There was more discussion in the following days until Mussolini entered the war. The British people and to some extent the British Government set their teeth and prepared to resist the German invasion that never came. But what difference was there between Lord Halifax and Sir Oswald Mosley, except that one was in Brixton Prison and the other was in the War Cabinet? As to R. A. Butler, Deputy Foreign Secretary, who was trying to enlist Sweden as an intermediary with Germany until the late summer, he, too, was a candidate for Brixton or should have been.

There is also criticism about the way the Second World War ended. Eisenhower is condemned for concentrating on southern Germany instead of marching on Berlin. At the very least he should have sent Montgomery marching on the Berlin road. If only this strategy had been followed the Russians would not have reached Berlin and there would have been no partition of Germany. These are wild ideas. There was tough fighting on the way to Berlin, fighting that Eisenhower preferred to avoid. What is more, Berlin had lost all significance as the capital of Germany. By the time the Russians reached it there was no German government in Berlin or anywhere else. No doubt Sir Oswald Mosley favoured a Western occupation of Berlin. Indeed I do not understand why he was not appointed Foreign Secretary instead of being locked up in Brixton or Holloway. It seems most unfair.

My autobiography has now reached America. It has had some odd reviews. A writer in the *New York Review of Books* has condemned me sharply for never having visited the United States and what is more for not intending ever to do so. Very odd. I can think of no reason for my ever going to the United States. I visit foreign countries either for the buildings or for the food. Neither of these reasons would justify a visit to the United States. There are plenty of other countries that I have not visited and that I regret not having been to. China obviously and Turkey-in-Asia; the Inca areas of Peru; Iceland. Nowadays I prefer to stay at home. But even if I felt an urge to travel it would not be to the United States. Another feature of this same reviewer is that he makes wild statements about me. For instance, he says all my six children were at public schools. The correct figure is: one. It is true that the school was Westminster, which perhaps counts for six.

I suppose that I should make some comments on public affairs since my last appearance. We have had four party conferences, which seems too much. I doubt whether they interest anybody except those who attend them. Maybe the SDP will die before next time; there seem to be quite enough parties without it. I suppose that Dr David Owen now regrets going over to the SDP. If he had remained in the Labour Party he would now be its leader. The Liberals put on a spirited performance to as little effect as ever. The Labour Party Conference was overshadowed by the question of who was to become leader. I understood that the question was settled from the start and it seems a great waste of time to make delegates come from all over the country merely to decide what had been decided already. At all events, no other decision of any moment was made. In the old days a leader of the Labour Party took years to mature. This time the Conference had a leader imposed on it of whom I at any rate had never heard.

The Labour Conference also put on its usual performance of giving an evasive answer to the question of nuclear weapons. Unilateral abandonment of nuclear weapons is the only policy that makes any sense and should be applied at once. It is also a policy that will never win a majority at a general election. This is a sad conclusion. I have a record as a champion for CND that goes back over twenty years. I dare say I could deliver as powerful a speech now as I did in those days of long ago: no one would take the slightest notice. CND has just had its greatest demonstration ever, both here and on the Continent. Nothing is going to happen. Indeed new consignments of the most malignant weapons are due to arrive any day. There will be more demonstrations and the weapons will be installed. Every day that passes brings nuclear war nearer, though no one can say how much nearer. I am beginning to think that I shall beat the race for nuclear war and die before the weapons go off. At any rate I have closed my mind to the problem.

That leaves me with the Conservative Conference. This is not a topic for serious consideration. It was a run of knockabout comedy. I have not known any Conference which spent its time on such futility. But perhaps this is the best way to run a Conference. No subject of any moment was debated. No decision of any moment was reached. Yet the Conservatives have gone home joyful. There seems some chance that the Thatcher Government may run into trouble, but this is taking too cheerful a view of contemporary affairs. If the bombs do not blow us up economic chaos will bring ruin upon us. One way or another we must take cover.

19

Prince Albert, Queen Victoria's husband, is doing well in his publicity at present, and well he deserves it. There is a fascinating exhibition devoted to him, a sort of glorified guide to the exhibition by Hermione Hobhouse, and a first-class biography by Robert Rhodes James. Albert took a long time to receive his deserts. Indeed I doubt whether he was fully appreciated during his lifetime. He was a foreigner. He disliked the rigmarole of court life and he was altogether too clever. The Great Exhibition of 1851, housed in the Crystal Palace, was inspired by Albert and he organised much of it down to the details. No British monarch has made such a contribution to British life. He was an outstanding architect in an amateur way. Both Osborne and Balmoral were largely his inspiration. Balmoral has remained the favourite country home of British monarchs to the present day and Osborne became Victoria's favourite in her latter years.

Most leading politicians disapproved of Albert at first and then came to appreciate him. This was true even of Palmerston, who was at feud with the Prince Consort for many years. Albert preserved peace between Great Britain and the United States shortly before his death. He had, too, an unrivalled record in his advocacy of social reform. He promoted working-class housing and municipal sanitation – activities which Victoria regarded with some disapproval. At the age of 11 he wrote in his Journal: 'I intend to train myself to be a good and useful man.' In this he succeeded. But his end was sad. For some undefined reason – perhaps a juvenile scrape of the Prince of Wales's, perhaps because of typhoid fever – he lost the will to live. At any rate he died, leaving Queen Victoria a widow for the last forty years of her reign.

Six years have passed since I gave my last television lecture. I could not think of any new subject, and in any case I was not wanted – an outmoded technique, no doubt. After some years I thought of a subject and have been trailing it around for some time. My last series of television lectures was called *How wars begin*. There was still a gap which I now propose to fill: *How wars end*. This will be more complicated than its predecessor. Most wars start in the same way: tension, misunderstanding and then a war. Some end by abrupt surrender, some by prolonged negotiations, some by a mixture of the two. What is more, even when the fighting stops, the agreement of peace can take a long time. In 1814–15 the Congress of Vienna went on for almost a year after Napoleon's abdication ended the fighting. The Treaty of Versailles came six months after the armistice. The other peace treaties that followed the First World War took even longer. The peace treaty with Italy came in 1947, though there had been unconditional surrender by Italy in 1943. The peace treaty with Japan was not concluded until 1951. Peace with Germany has never been concluded at all for the simple reason that Germany in the old sense ceased to exist in 1945. What delightful complications lie ahead of me. I must sound one warning. I suffer among other things from nominal amnesia, a high-flown name for forgetfulness. Short-lived, I may say – the name or date comes back to me within a few minutes. But I can hardly stand staring at the camera for all that time. I can't think what to do. Make something up, I suppose.

There is a serious trouble in my life quite apart from Parkinson's disease: books are getting too long, and there are too many of them, usually at certain times of the year. For some months I had no books at all to review. Then monstrous tomes came in shoals. For instance, one day recently I received three books on Field Marshal Montgomery to review: one of four hundred pages, one of nearly five hundred and one of nearly nine hundred. It is an accusation commonly directed at reviewers that they do not read the books they get or at best pass their hands lightly over the cover and wait for inspiration. I am more conscientious. Having no regular occupation except shopping, I sit at home day after day going loyally through my assignment until I have read the lot. But it certainly leaves me with very little spare time. Now I thought the moment had arrived when I could get on with some other writing or even read a book for pleasure. I rejoiced too soon. What awaits me today? A book of virtually nine hundred pages on F. E. Smith, first

Earl of Birkenhead, by John Campbell, has appeared on my desk this morning. John Campbell has written first-rate biographies. I even have a vague recollection that F. E. Smith, Lord Birkenhead, was once a figure of some political importance, probably a man just too clever to reach the highest point. I suppose I must settle down with the book for the next three weeks. But I can't. This morning a photographer is coming, I can't think why. Then I am recording my second instalment of *How wars end*. After that, some BBC agents are coming to record my views on the First World War, not that I have any. I have really reached the stage of asking about the First World War: 'What was that?' How terrible it seemed at the time, and how trivial it seems now compared with what is coming. I even have people ringing me up and asking what the Third World War will be like. I answer: 'Wait and see. When the Third World War comes you won't know. You'll be dead.' So I had better get back to F. E. Smith while I have time.

I have more serious complaints in life than the excessive length of books that I have to review. Among the most troublesome and certainly the most exasperating is noise. This is the price of living in modern times. One curse, rarely commented on, is the helicopters that fly persistently over North London. Not only do they fly over my garden: the same helicopter flies over it again and again. What are they doing? I am told that for some obscure reason they are observing the traffic and reporting where there are traffic jams. I don't believe a word of it. They fly around for sheer pleasure, happy in the knowledge that they are making life unbearable. But still worse is the music which goes on ceaselessly. For instance, this morning I was taken to the television studio in a hired car. There was canned music all the time, occasionally interrupted by conversations between the driver and his office, replete with mysterious assignments. Then the music starts again. My wife tells me that in Oxford Street the shops have canned music going on all the time, acute enough to threaten her with a heart attack. Then, on a more domestic level, there is on the other side of our street a family with three or four young men. They all have cars equipped with radios and the radios play all the time. If one of them comes home he parks his car outside my window and leaves the radio playing, sometimes all night. Since I sleep with my bedroom window open, I have a restless night. Occasionally they have a party, at least once a month. Then the radio plays until two o'clock in the morning. Soon I expect they will be playing their radios simultaneously on and on and on. If I try to escape the radios by walking on Hampstead Heath I am pursued, indeed surrounded, by young boys or girls carrying voluble radios with them in the quietest areas. I have known radios played in railway carriages and of course in public houses. Their public playing should be made illegal.

Twenty years ago I published a book about the origins of the Second World War. At the time it was dismissed as wrong-headed and controversial. Now it has become the accepted version for most people. But there still lurks some trouble in the book, particularly the so-called Hossbach Protocol. I asserted that this document was a forgery, an assertion which caused much indignation. Now after many years a Berlin lawyer called Dankwart Kluge has taken another look at the Hossbach Protocol. His conclusions are startling. The Hossbach Protocol never existed as a formal document. Indeed it probably never existed in any form. Two documents were submitted to the Nuremberg Tribunal: one was an English translation, markedly longer than the alleged Protocol, the other a microfilm copy of a microfilm. However, the Tribunal accepted these documents. They were held to prove that Hitler was planning an aggressive war. On the strength of them, Goering was condemned to death and only escaped the hangman by taking poison. No evidence that Hitler planned aggressive war has ever been produced. Hossbach, who is alleged to have compiled the so-called protocol, was from the first an associate of the German generals who opposed Hitler's policy or tried to.

The revision upsets the entire verdict of the Nuremberg Tribunal, which is still solemnly quoted as justification of the Allied war against Germany. It would be going too far to suggest that Great Britain and France started the Second World War by declaring it, but they did declare it all the same.

I spent most of last Sunday watching the silent movie *Napoleon*, made by Abel Gance some fifty years ago. The scenes of the French Revolution seem to me very unlikely: the principal characters make very strange faces and wear very rough clothing. Napoleon specialises in rushing from the left-hand side of the screen to the right and back again: he always seems in a hurry, no doubt

154

seeking a further opportunity to pull faces. The film is very funny and occasionally very dramatic. It is very exciting. But really it won't do. I may have been too corrupted by watching talkies to be able to tell, but I doubt whether it is a masterpiece even as a silent movie. Of course it is much better than most of the talking masterpieces we have been offered in recent times. You have only to think of *Reds* to appreciate what the cinema can now make of revolutions.